Wild Spirits

Running with the Herd

a novel by

Ann Clemons

ISBN-13: 978-0615808185

Equine Arts
P.O. Box 235
San Cristobal, NM 87564
ann@annclemons.com

Dedicated with Love, Gratitude and Joy
to the horses that have inspired me.
You bring so much joy to the world!
and
To all aspiring Wild Spirits.
May you find your Dreams.

1

GEORGE

The man walked around all four sides of the enclosure. He frowned, squinting into the sun. *Will this one even live?* he wondered. He leaned over and looked between the bars of the fence panel and felt a flash of irritation. The horse's belly was raw and bleeding where flies had congregated and fed. There was no shade to shield him from the blazing hot desert sun, and therefore nothing to deter the flies and other insects that swarmed around the government livestock pens.

George was familiar with the scene. Every time the government brought out their helicopters to round up these wild horses, there were some that didn't make it. Often they died of fright, or broke a leg in the frantic run that ensued from the chase. *Those might well be the lucky ones,* thought George. He stood up and looked into the eyes of the stallion. Swollen from the heat and the flies, his misery was evident and George felt that he could actually see the life draining from what was once a proud, beautiful creature.

"Wonder if that one will even make it to the truck?"

The voice sounded all too familiar, and sure enough, George turned to see Jack, the killer buyer who frequented the live stock auctions and these round ups. His cap bearing the logo of the local feed store was pushed back on his head, and George could see a tan line across his forehead from hours spent in the sun.

Killer buying was pretty lucrative as far as the livestock business goes, but Jack's dirty faded jeans and denim shirt did not reflect his prosperity. He liked to keep a low profile, it was part of the game.

George nodded his head in greeting. He had known Jack since high school. Jack's dad had owned a business in town, while George had grown up on the family ranch. Aside from sports, they had never run in the same circles, and had never been the best of friends. Jack wasn't a bad guy or anything, but he had always been the one looking to make a fast buck, and had chosen a profession where the dollar counted more than the lives he was gambling with.

"How goes it, Jack?"

"Y'know, I used to try to keep count of how many of these Ole hides they were rounding up outta these parts, but I've hauled off so many now I've given up keeping track. How're things out at the ranch, George? Picking up any?"

"Aw, we're doing alright, Jack." George glanced up toward the mesa top. "A little bit of rain would sure go a long way right now, though."

"I hear that! It's been a long dry spell." Jack looked at the stallion again. The horse hadn't moved. "Well, ain't much left of him, but he ought to go cheap anyway. Guess I'd better go get my number, this show's fixen to start. Later George."

"Later, Jack." George squinted into the sun, watching the tall, robust buyer head for the office. He turned back to the stallion. "Tough luck, old boy. I wouldn't want to be in your shoes," he mumbled under his breath. Then his eyebrows shot up as he thought he noticed an almost imperceptible flicker in the stallion's eye. *Maybe this one's not quite done yet*, he thought. George looked at the horse a second or two, then shrugged and walked off toward the sale ring.

He didn't think the future looked bright for that horse. The whole band had been rounded up because many of the ranchers in the area had felt that the horses were a liability. In this drought they wanted what little grass there was for their cattle. The government had come in and rounded up the whole herd, which had consisted of mares, foals, some yearlings, and of course, the stallion. Many of the youngsters would go to homes. They were young enough to be trainable. But an older stallion, well, he just didn't fit in anywhere, and there was a good chance that he would die, unable to make the adjustment to captivity.

George felt a surge of empathy for the wild creature. Not fitting in had always been George's specialty, and he had often walked the path of a loner, being more interested in keeping the land and the wildlife safe instead of always looking for better ways to cut the costs of caring for livestock. He didn't mind that he was a little different, hell, that was how he had gotten his wife Sally. He smiled a little at the thought as he entered the sale barn.

The stallion eyed the man looking at him through the fence rails. He had lost interest in most of what was going on; he was too tired and hungry and thirsty to care. But something about that two-legged creature demanded his attention. It seemed important, so he watched, without moving. When the two–legged moved away, the stallion sighed; he knew there was no point in looking in the feeder, which was empty, or the water tank. The water had something dead floating in it that had turned it rancid, so he returned to his almost coma-like state, staring out across the foothills that had once been his home. The rolling foothills rose toward the mountain peaks where he and his mares had roamed free. A searing pain in his gut broke through the haze, and his knees began to tremble. Eventually the wave of pain passed, and just as the stallion was slipping back into his cloudy otherworld, a two–legged came and put a rope around his neck.

"Hell, Joe, I don't know if we can get this one through the ring 'fore he drops."

"We have to try though. Ya know how pissed off they get if they have to haul off a carcass." Joe wrapped the rope around the horn of his saddle and spurred his mount forward. They dragged the stallion, stumbling and choking, toward the sale ring.

The auctioneer eyed the horse that the riders were dragging through the gate.

"Here we go ladies and gentlemen, one that anyone can afford to own." He rolled his eyes at the killer buyers, signaling them that this would be short and sweet, and they would be on to bigger and better horseflesh in a moment.

George looked up from the sales list that he had been reading, to see the stallion stumble into the ring. He sighed deeply, knowing what the ensuing sale would be like. Cocking his big gray Stetson back on his head, he wiped his brow and looked expectantly at the auctioneer.

"Five dollars, do I hear five dollars anyone?" The crowd was silent. "Come on now, ya'll. Only five dollars, and you can take this real live mustang home. Own a piece of the Wild West." The silence seemed to echo through the barn, and was Jack's cue. He raised his number and nodded his head. The horse wouldn't bring much, even for glue, but at five bucks Jack could afford to take the chance.

"Five dollars," rapped out the auctioneer. "Five dollars, going once, going twice."

George watched as the horse stumbled again, going down on his knees. "God dammit," he mumbled under his breath and then stood up.

"Six dollars, Dick. Six dollars."

"SOLD!" The auctioneer rapped his gavel on the wood in front of him. He wasn't going to waste any more time on this bag of bones. He had over 100 more horses to sell this afternoon. The pen riders moved in to drag the stallion out of the ring.

"I'll take him, boys," George said as he motioned them to wait, then climbed through the rails into the ring and took the rope from the pen riders. All the while he was thinking, *what the hell is wrong with me? I need another horse like a hole in the head, especially one that'll most likely die 'fore I can get him home.*

"Climb on up there and ride 'em out George," the auctioneer said, laughing. "We've got more critters to get through here today!"

Ignoring the banter, George slowly and carefully helped the horse shuffle out the gate. As they hobbled along the lane in the direction of his truck and trailer, George used the opportunity to look over his newest purchase.

The stallion had sores on his shoulders and hips where he had probably run into the gatepost as he was driven into the catch pens during the round up. Of course nobody had so much as cleaned the sores out, much less treated them in any way. The flies were having a field day. His long, black, once flowing mane and tail were knotted and full of mattes, and he had dried, green manure stains on his silvery red roan coat where he had finally lay down in his exhaustion.

George's rig was easy to spot among the crowd in the dusty back lot. Oxidized paint on the hood and dents caused by years of dirt roads and livestock hauling made it stand out from the expensive, new rigs driven by most of the other buyers. Among the horse people, rigs were a status symbol; the bigger and more expensive, the better they liked it.

"Humph," George muttered as he and the stallion shuffled along, stopping every few steps. The stallion did not know about halters and ropes and leading so forward progress was slowed even more as man and horse tried to figure each other out. He had much more important things to spend his money on than expensive trucks and fancy trailers. Then he chuckled as he thought, *Yeah, like nearly dead wild horses!*

Before trying to load the horse in the trailer, George got him a bucket of cool, clean, water, allowing him to only drink a few sips at a time so his parched innards wouldn't cramp up. Then he threw some clean hay in the trailer so the horse could munch a little on the way home if he felt like it.

The loading took a little time. The stallion was so weak, and the trailer an unfamiliar object. Had he been fresh off the range, the job would have been a lot tougher. But he had little energy for objections, and George had lots of patience, so they were soon on their way.

The stallion braced himself as the trailer bumped and swayed down the dirt road. The water George had given him before they left was starting to work it's magic on his system, and he was perking up ever so little. There was hay on the floor of the trailer, but he was still very weak, and it required most of his focus just to keep his balance, so he only took an occasional nibble. Now that his soft tissue was somewhat hydrated, his senses began to come alive. What had happened to his mares? He had tried his best to protect them, but they were gone. There was an aching, hollow feeling deep inside him that had nothing to do with his physical condition. He had not seen them since having been separated at the sale barn. He had wanted to lie down and die there; to escape the hopelessness and the pain, but this two–legged had not let that happen. So the stallion waited. What else was there but the waiting?

Sally's going to have my hide, thought George as he steered the rig through the potholes on the sun-baked ranch road. We don't have enough hay up for the ranch horses as it is, and these drought prices are killing us. We don't even have pasture to turn the old boy out in. I didn't come home with that replacement heifer that I was supposed to be buying either.

He grimaced at the thought of what his wife was going to say when he got home, then he smiled. Sally was his best friend, his business partner, and the love of his life. She was also the one that kept the ranch business afloat and his feet on the ground. They had known each other since high school, and she was well aware that practicality was not always his strong suite.

His thoughts shifted to the other new addition to their ranch; Elena. He sighed. Elena had come to live with them a few weeks ago. He and Sally had no children of their own and had decided to open up their lives and their home to one in need. She was an orphaned teen from the reservation. Her parents had been killed 7 years ago, and she had gone from foster home to foster home, finding it difficult to fit in anywhere; and the older she got, the harder it had been for Child Welfare to find someone to take her. As George thought about Elena, her image formed in his thoughts and he was momentarily startled by what he saw. Her eyes had the same vacant, hopeless look that he had seen in the stallion. *I guess that isn't so surprising,* he thought. They have both suffered terrible loss. George's attention returned fully to his driving as the road turned to dirt and potholes.

The sky was cloudy and blowing a hot dry breeze when George pulled in the ranch gate. Sally walked out to meet him as he pulled up in front of the barn. She raised her eyebrows when she saw what was in the trailer and stepped forward for a closer look. Sally's eyes met the stallion's, and what she saw there caused a single tear to slowly slide down her freckled cheek. She looked at her husband, who was watching her apprehensively.

"Well," she said, brushing a piece of curly red hair out of her eyes. "I guess we better get him unloaded and find him some grub."

Some time later, as they stood leaning on the top rail of the corral fence, George sighed.

"I couldn't leave him there, Sally. He would have gone with Jack Miller."

Sally frowned. The thought of any animal going to the killer made her stomach lurch. She knew that her husband could not have let this one go.

"I know. Sometimes..." she sighed. "Well, He must have been incredible when he was running with his mares. Do you think he will survive this way? In captivity, without his mares or his freedom?"

"Hard to tell, darlin'. The best we can do is give him a chance."

As George spoke, he looked again into the stallion's eyes and thought he saw a spark of life there, and maybe something more. Then he felt the small splash of a raindrop as it hit his cheek.

2

ELENA

What am I going to do? I can't get rid of the pain! All of this change, this confusion, nobody understands how I feel, not even me! Her anxiety level rose with each thought, and not even the heavy exertion of climbing the steep rocky incline seemed tiring enough to take the edge off. She pushed herself harder, the muscles in her lean, tan arms bulging with the effort of pulling herself up that rock face and over the precipice onto the ledge. Having reached the top, she collapsed on the flat rock, lying still in the hot breeze, concentrating on restoring oxygen to her lungs and body.

The act of lying still seemed to generate more activity in her thoughts. She groaned. What should she do? Try as she may, Elena could not seem to find a rational way out of her misery. The more she tried to come up with a solution, the more hopelessness welled up inside her. The mid summer sun was unfiltered by clouds, making it very intense, and instead of having a cooling effect, the breeze was even hotter. She continued to lie motionless in the heat, willing her thoughts elsewhere, anywhere, to escape her misery. She drifted for a while, floating above herself, separate from that young, tormented teen, and landed in her childhood home on the reservation.

The corners of her lips curved slightly in a smile as she saw her mother sweeping the wooden steps leading to the door of their small adobe home. Her mother had been tiny, and a little bit round, and to her, cleanliness had not been a choice, it had been a lifestyle. Elena sighed, but otherwise remained motionless on the rock as her mind and spirit wandered through a different and happier time and place. She could see the cedar pole corrals where her father had kept his livestock. In a shady corner by the three-sided lean-to stood Sam, her father's old Appaloosa and her best childhood friend. Softness seemed to melt her anxiety as she remembered old Sam. She had spent many hours sharing her childhood thoughts and dreams with that horse. He had been a wise, gentle soul and would stand quietly, his ears cocked as though listening, as little Elena had sat on his bony old back, her arms wrapped around his neck, pouring out her deepest secrets and feelings. Never then, as a child, had she felt the chilling emptiness of being so completely alone as she did now, at what seemed like the ripe old age of seventeen.

She shivered. A cloud had passed over the sun, and she felt as though cold fingers had brushed across her face, dragging her spirit away from those happy times, bringing her back to the present. Heaving a sigh, she sat up and looked around her. From her perch on the rock, she could see for miles. The heat waves distorted the air between her ledge and the mountains in the East, giving her surroundings an otherworldly effect. Elena turned and looked into the cedar and scrub oak that rambled into the rocky hills behind the place where she sat. *Bet I could just disappear forever here,* she thought. *Just start walking, and fade away into the desert. No one would ever find me. Hell, no one would even bother to try.* That thought brought her fully back to her pain, and she jumped to her feet. The hot breeze ruffled her long, black hair as she headed for the minimal shade of the stunted, twisted cedar trees. The dry native desert grass crunched under her boots as she walked, carefully avoiding the scattered cactus and buffalo grass. Moving felt good now that she had recovered from her climb, and she decided to explore her surroundings.

The reality of her situation, her pain, and her confusion crept back into her thoughts as she walked. Elena shook her head as if trying to ward it off, even as she realized she had to come fully into the present and decide what to do with her life. *Lonely,* she thought, *lonely, dark, and hopeless.* Those were the best words that she could think of to describe the past seven years of her existence.

Since her parents had died in that car wreck when she was ten, her life had consisted of moving from one foster home to the next. Her brother had been killed in the war, and her only living relative was an alcoholic uncle, her father's brother. Even if he had wanted her, which he didn't, the Child Welfare Department would not have placed Elena there. Everything she knew had been there on the reservation, but she had been placed with a white family in Phoenix. The confusion of being transplanted to the city only compounded the shock of losing her family, her home, and her beloved Sam. Her pace quickened as though she could escape the memories.

Elena's heart had been broken, but her spirit was still intact. The family she had been placed with was OK as far as white families go, and they had tried their best to make her feel welcome. But Elena might as well have been placed in a foreign country for all that she didn't understand about the new life she had been booted into. Everything about it was strange to her, and the grief that she carried threatened to overwhelm her. She missed her freedom terribly. The freedom of walking under the stars and hearing the coyotes sing and the owls call. The freedom of running through the cactus and the rocks, feeling the wind in her hair while racing the jackrabbits. There wasn't even anyone around that could speak her native language, and the teachers at school actually discouraged her from speaking in her native tongue. As she thought about that, waves of emotions washed over her. She was again feeling the pain and confusion of having what was left of her childhood stripped from her. And there was no way to adequately express her feelings without using the language of her childhood and of her people.

Desperately lonely, she had slipped out one night through the bedroom window and had attempted to hitchhike back to the reservation. Even if there was no family there for her, she was sure that the familiarity of the desert, the land of her people, would help to thin the cloud of loneliness and desperation that had settled over her. She had never arrived there, however. The police had picked her up early the following morning, and it was decided that she should be farther away from everything she was familiar with in hopes of deterring her from running again.

This time Elena was sent to Albuquerque, another city; a place loud enough to drown out the sounds of her childhood. The call of the hawk and the singing of the breeze through the trees. Life was chipping away at her soul, and the changes brought on by puberty only compounded the difficulties for a young teen with no real ties to the world. Rather than subsiding, her grief had burrowed into a corner of her heart and hardened there. She carried it with her always, but had learned how to keep it hidden. Others saw her as a very serious child that no one could connect with. Her foster family in Albuquerque, despairing of ever getting through her hard shell, had finally given up. Elena was moved again, this time to a ranch in the New Mexico desert.

Elena had gazed out the window of the car that transported her to her new home. She felt the stirrings of interest and recognition in her heart. *Finally, something I understand,* she thought. As she looked out across the miles of high desert grass to the rocky mesa, she had felt a tiny spark begin to glow, showing the first signs of life. Looking at the bright blue sky as the car sped down the ranch road, Elena had wondered what might be next for her in this new but hauntingly familiar place.

As she continued her exploration of the mesa top, Elena felt a touch on her arm. Startled, she turned to see who the intruder was and found that it was only the branch of a pretty little pine tree. She decided to pause here for a rest and sat against the tree trunk, comfortable in the shade. As she looked around, her thoughts returned to her latest foster family.

George and Sally Layton owned a small ranch and had no children of their own. Elena soon learned that they had decided to take in an older child that could help with the chores around the place. George had thought that a girl might be some company for his wife. As beautiful as that desert wilderness was, it could be a lonely place at times. Although Elena had not been able to open her heart and feel close to the Laytons, they had been kind to her and treated her fairly. Most importantly, at least from Elena's standpoint, they had provided her with comfort of the outdoors and open spaces. This was a freedom that she had not experienced since her parents died. Even many of her chores were pleasurable because she was often helping with the livestock, especially the ranch horses. Everything seemed pretty decent in her life, she thought, considering.

But as she sat under her tree lost in contemplation, the anxiety began to creep back, like a tremor running up her spine and lodging in her head. *It's WRONG*, she thought. *It's wrong, there's a huge piece missing, and I don't know what or why, or how to fix it! I don't know what to do. If only mother were here!* THERE ... she had said it. There it was, the whole problem in a nutshell. Her mother wasn't there, her father wasn't there, and they never would be. Nobody was there to listen, no shoulder to cry on. Elena shivered. *I'm completely ALONE*, she wailed silently. As the despair washed over her, Elena's eyes caught sight of something. Her thoughts quieted as her focus riveted on the object her roving eyes had found.

Elena slowly stood up, afraid to take her eyes off the object, in case it should disappear. As she gently pried it loose from under the cactus where it was lodged, her heart began to beat faster. The design on this old piece of pottery was quite simple and very beautiful. The lines and patterns that decorated this pot had a rhythm to them that felt balanced and graceful. The edges of the sherd were smooth and rounded from centuries of sand and rain and wind. Elena's eyes traveled forward and up. She could hardly contain her excitement. There was a good chance that this ancient piece of pottery had been washed down hill by the last rain. As her gaze traveled through the trees, she caught sight of a small, rocky slope.

Slowly, she began to climb, her eyes searching every step of the way. As she reached out for a handhold to help pull herself up, she felt a smooth object under her hand. Another piece of pottery! The design was not so elaborate on this piece, and it was heavier, more like an everyday utility sort of pot, and probably much older than the first piece she had found. Elena's excitement grew, and she continued her climb, her mind picturing the people that had crafted these pots and lived here so long ago. She reached the top, stopped suddenly, and caught her breath. She looked around her, she almost felt nauseous from all of the emotions churning inside of her. This was it! She had found it! This ancient village of the People, her ancestors. The Power Place that her mother had told her stories about as a child.

She wanted to see everything at once, and had to calm herself so that she could take in all the details of this wonderful place. There were interconnected dirt mounds that covered a large piece of the area; the foundations of what had once been a series of living spaces. Even though time, vegetation, and erosion had taken its toll, Elena could still clearly see the layout of what had probably once been a thriving village. Slowly, her eyes wandered across the site, taking in every detail. As anxious as she was to cover every bit of this newfound treasure, to see every item that remained of this ancient place, there was something else she needed to do first. This was that special piece of the earth that connected with her heart as though it was her own. Her soul felt as if it had lived here forever, and even though she had never been here physically, the place seemed familiar. Tears welled up in her eyes as she remembered those evenings around the fire, the stories her mother had told of the ancients and their teachings. Sobbing, she sank to her knees, grasping handfuls of the dry, sandy earth and letting it run through her fingers.

When the tears had run their course, Elena took in the sight before her. This was a sacred place. She could feel it. Here were ruins that dated back perhaps 800 years or more. She could still see the scars on the hillsides where "The People" had pulled up the rocks they had used build their villages. After sitting for a time with her memories, Elena stood and looked around. Where should she start? The foundations were still here, and she could see a large circle that might have been a meeting place. As she wandered through the ancient village, she was careful where she placed her feet. She did not want to trespass against the ancients that had once lived here.

A cry from above pierced her thoughts, and she looked up to see a hawk circling, soaring, and dipping on the air currents. She could hear her mother's voice as though they were in the same room. "Be still Elena, listen. Brother hawk has a message just for you if you will only stop and listen." Elena sat on a rock and closed her eyes, waiting to see what would happen. Images began to gently push their way into her thoughts. Memories of her mother and father, their home on the reservation, teachings of "The People" that her mother had started instilling in Elena when she was just a baby. It felt as though someone had wrapped a warm blanket around her shoulders and was gently rocking her. For the first time in five years she felt, safe, secure, and loved. Gently, but firmly, the message pushed it's way into her consciousness, leaving no room for doubt.

As Elena watched the hawk disappear toward the Western horizon, she felt a raindrop hit her cheek, mingling with the salt from her recent tears. She had been so intent on her thoughts and memories, she had failed to notice the clouds that had moved in. *I must hurry*, she thought. *I will be late for evening chores.* Extending a silent Thank You to the hawk, she gave herself a minute to be fully back in the present. Breathing a sigh of disappointment, she looked around again at this new found treasure and vowed to return as soon as possible. Feeling another raindrop, she turned and started down the slope.

As she came running down the lane, Elena could see George already busy with the evening chores. She smiled shyly, taking George by surprise. In the few weeks Elena had been with them, he had rarely seen her smile.

"Sally and I were beginning to worry, Elena. You don't normally stay away so late." He handed her a bucket of grain to take to the horses. He was full of questions, but he kept them to himself, not wanting to intrude on whatever was the cause of that smile.

"We have a new addition to the family, Elena. When you are done feeding the horses, I'd like you to meet him. I think the two of you might have a lot in common."

Elena grimaced. *Great*, she thought. With all of the incredible things she had swirling around in her head right now, she was not in the mood to be polite to some stranger. And what did George mean, a new family addition?

Usually Elena spent more time than was needed while feeding the horses. She liked to speak to each one and spend time being with them. Today she just gave each a greeting and a cursory pat, and then headed back to the main barn. Her head was still full of visions from her day's journey, but George's words kept intruding on her thoughts making it difficult to focus on them. *Oh, why did they have to pick today to bring home a stranger?* she moaned silently. All she really wanted to do was get dinner over with so that she could go to her room and relive the wonderful events of the afternoon.

George scratched his head as he watched Elena head for the horse barn to do her chores. There was a slight spring to her step that he had not seen before, and the smile she had greeted him with seemed a brand new addition to her normal, serious facial expressions. *Now what has gotten into that girl*, he thought. Tipping his sweat-stained Stetson back, he rubbed his forehead absently as he thought about the past few weeks. Elena had only been at the ranch such a short time, but he and Sally were beginning to worry that they might never crack through the hard shell that had formed around Elena's heart. She was a good girl, always doing what she was told, and never calling attention to herself. She seemed more like a robot than a teenage girl, moving mechanically through her days, showing no outward emotion, never calling attention to herself, and showing no evidence of dreams or expectations of life.

She is a loner, he thought. *Guess I collect them!* Chuckling, George pictured his wife, Sally. She too had been a loner. Even though she had been raised right here in ranch country, she had a compassion for the livestock and wild animals that had seemed excessive and unnatural to most of the kids they hung with in school. Sally's circle of friends had always been small but select, and she had never seemed to mind that the others found her to be so different. Indeed, this difference was the very quality that had attracted George to her in the first place. He sighed. Too bad one of them wasn't more practical though, since they were in the cattle business. The branding and shipping was always a difficult time for the both of them.

George ambled over to the corral that he and Sally had built for the stallion. Resting his arms over the top rail, he sighed as he looked again at the poor condition of this wild, once beautiful creature. Noticing the horse's vacant expression, it occurred to George that it was the same way Elena had looked when she had arrived at the ranch. It was almost as though their souls had left for parts unknown, leaving an empty shell behind. *Kindred spirits*, he thought. *Just like me and Sally.*

Hearing the soft shuffling and banging noises in the barn indicating that Elena was done with her chores, George strode off to find her. He would be very interested to see what effect, if any, the stallion might have on Elena. Given this new, lighter mood that she seemed to be in tonight, George felt that this might be a very interesting meeting. He stuck his head around the corner and saw Elena putting the feed scoops in the barrel.

"I see I am just in time," he said. "Why don't you come with me now and meet our new friend?"

Elena nodded and without a word followed George out of the barn. As they rounded the corner, she noticed that some new fence panels had been set in the clearing under the big cottonwood tree. As they moved closer to the clearing she saw a horse standing in the shadows under the tree. Her back straightened at the sight, and she wore an intense expression on her face as they approached the corral. Without stopping, Elena climbed between the fence rails and walked slowly to the center of the corral. Barely breathing, she stood perfectly still as the stallion turned to look at her. The two of them stood just that way, scattered raindrops going unnoticed, for several minutes as George looked on. Somewhere nearby he heard a door open and close, and soon Sally was quietly standing next to him. Even though neither the girl nor the horse was moving, it was obvious to George and Sally that some sort of communication going on between them. Elena's back was straight and motionless, and the stallion's head was up, his ears pricked forward, his nostrils flared as he sniffed her scent.

Elena began to tremble inside as she felt the wall around her soul begin to crumble. She looked at the stallion and thought, *You have been where I have been. We are in the same prison, and have the same wall around us.*

As George and Sally silently watched, the stallion lowered his head and released the breath that he seemed to have been holding. His whole body relaxed, and his glassy eyes took on a new, softer look. Elena had her back to them, but they were able to see her shoulders drop as she released some built up tension. Her stance went from one of tense isolation to relaxed expectation. Aside from these slight signs, neither girl nor horse moved, but George and Sally could feel the underlying current running between the two—a non-verbal communication that said so much more than words ever could. The two observers looked at each other, and with a silent communication of their own, moved away quietly toward the house, leaving the loners alone with their emotion.

Looking carefully at this new two-legged, the stallion struggled with an intense knot of images and feelings that he was unfamiliar with. In his world, the unfamiliar could easily mean danger. He sniffed the air looking for the scent of anything that might signal the need for flight, but the only familiar scents he could detect were that of the rain, and the stronger smell of human presence, which was not at all new or surprising anymore. There was still confusion, however. This two-legged was female, and he could feel an intensity and excitement emanating from her that he had not felt from any other. Her presence brought vivid images of his mares, wildness, and freedom to mind, instead of the strangeness and detachment that he had felt from other humans. He felt his muscles twitch with the memories of running free over the plains and through the trees. He could smell the wildflowers and the green mountain grass and the bubbling brooks of the old high country summer range. He waited.

Elena was captivated. This poor emaciated stallion had been wild and free, just as she had; she could feel his wildness. Her heart pounded and her shallow breathing quickened and deepened a bit as the stallion flicked his ears toward her and breathed sharply. For a moment, she could see a change deep in his eyes. Through the cloudy dullness that had protected the depths of his feeling came a spark of light. As she watched, the spark grew to a small flame of what seemed like recognition.

Elena and the stallion stood there, charged with electricity, for what only seemed like a moment. A sudden *Whoosh*, directly overhead, broke the spell. Elena looked up to see an owl settling into the tree above the stallion and realized that the sky had grown dark, the light drizzle was turning to a harder rain, and that more time had passed than she had thought. She could still feel the adrenaline running through her from the unexpected meeting, and she struggled to regain her composure as the stallion turned away.

It's your time to hunt, Owl, Elena smiled at the tree where the huge bird blended into the darkness. *And it's time for me to go inside. Good night, horse, I will see you in my dreams.* Elena watched him, but he seemed to have returned to his former state of detachment.

As Elena neared the house, wonderful scents permeated her dream state, floating in the damp air. Dinner! She had not even thought of eating! Her stomach was rumbling, and thoughts of stallions and owls gave way to stew and dumplings as she climbed the two steps to the door. Taking a deep breath, she readied herself to leave her world of nature and spirits and rejoin the humans. George and Sally would be waiting, and she was quite late for the evening meal.

3

HAWK

Lying in bed that night, Sally lay listening to the peaceful sounds of George's breathing as he slept and the quiet hissing of the rain on the tin roof. The knot in her stomach that Sally felt each time she stepped out the door onto the drought-stricken, crunchy brown native grass finally began to loosen and unravel. She could almost feel the earth breath a sigh of relief as her pores absorbed the fresh moisture falling on her dry, parched soil.

The relief brought by the rain seemed to extend far beyond what it brought to the plants and soil, Sally mused. The image of Elena and the stallion floated through her mind. The hard edges of that wild pair had seemed to melt away as George and Sally had stood watching in the early evening drizzle. No one would ever know for sure what had gone on between Elena and that horse, but Sally recognized the tie between the two wild creatures that had stood motionless in that corral, and she knew that something very powerful had happened for them through that meeting. When Elena had come into the house for supper, there had been a peaceful calm aura about her that had been missing before. The girl had quietly eaten her stew and dumpling before apologizing and excusing herself from the table. She had worn a slight smile, and what Sally interpreted as a look of quiet wonder on her face as she climbed the stairs to her room.

George and Sally had stayed up for awhile listening to the rain.

Neither one of them had wanted to go to bed and lose these moments of misty, peaceful bliss. Practicality finally overtook their dream world, and knowing that they had their usual early chores to do in the morning, they had headed for bed.

Sally snuggled deeper into her pillows next to her sleeping husband, and with visions of girls and horses and rain floating through her hazy mind, she finally surrendered to much-needed sleep.

Whoo hoo, whoo hoo. Elena lay in her bed listening to Owl's voice mingling with the hiss and gurgle of the rain on the roof and running in the gutters outside her window. *Better than a lullaby*, she thought, smiling as her drowsy mind floated through memories of her day. It seemed that she had been parched, like the desert around her, for such a long time. Until today she had felt like she would dry up and wither away. New life seemed to be trickling into her just as the rivulets of rainwater trickled into the cracks of the hard dry earth.

Unwilling to release the memories and pictures that the day had turned loose in her mind, Elena wanted to stay awake and try to absorb it all. But soon her thoughts began to cloud, and sleep overtook her.

Dawn. The clouds slowly parted and then disappeared as red and pink and gold painted the Eastern horizon minutes before the sun began to peek through the juniper and pinion trees on the rise east of the house. The sunrays twinkled as they passed through the remaining raindrops on the tree branches and ground growth. That strong, tough native grass was beginning to show a tint of green already. It always amazed George that no matter how long it seemed to lie dry and dormant, the minute there was a decent rain the grass filled with the green life given by water and sun. His thoughts turned to more practical things as he stood on the porch steps sipping his coffee. Was this rain just a fluke? Will the pasture grass see enough growth to supply food for the livestock? *Please*, he thought as he looked to the sky, *send enough moisture to keep things green and growing through the rest of the season!* On the desert, as dry as it was, it only took one month of summer rains to create enough growth for winter pasture. This was called the monsoon season and there had not been a good one for two years. He tried to not even consider the possibility that the drought would return full-force and extinguish the hope that was beginning to grow in his heart.

Drought had been known to last for decades in this high desert country, and many ranchers had succumbed to depleted bank accounts and the necessity of having to sell their livestock, their livelihood, and move to nearby cities for jobs.

Not wanting to think about such negative possibilities, George reached back inside by the door, traded his coffee mug for the sweat-stained Stetson, stepped off the porch, and headed for the barn knowing he would find comfort in the constancy of doing the morning chores.

As George walked toward the barn, a slight sound caught his attention. He stopped to listen. Looking in the direction of the stallion's corral, he saw Elena was well ahead of him this morning and was feeding the stallion. She was absorbed with something and didn't notice George, so he decided not to call attention to himself and went on to the barn. The ranch horses were already munching their breakfast as well. Smiling and thoughtful, he went out to the hay barn to load the cattle hay on the feed truck. After breakfast he would drive to the field where he was keeping the cattle as they waited for pasture and drop piles of the precious hay for the cows. Usually hay was only fed in the winter months and his heart always thumped harder when he had to break into the winter stores this time of year.

The stallion eyed Elena from across the pen as she climbed through the rails of the fence and set the flakes of hay on the ground. She stepped back quietly and checked to make sure there was plenty of clean water in the tank Sally had placed by the gutter spout to catch the rainwater. It was clear and full and had overflowed during the night creating a muddy place around the tank. *Good*, she thought, *his hooves must be terribly dry. Having to step in the mud to get to the water will help to ease the dryness.*

Elena had planned her chores so that feeding the stallion would be the last she had to do. Now she could spend a little time getting better acquainted. Sleep had come easily and swiftly the night before and she felt more rested than she had since her parents had died. She had not spent much time in that hazy otherworld between sleep and wakefulness. Memories of the previous day were stampeding through her brain like a herd of wild horses the moment she opened her eyes.

Many emotions, long buried under that rock hard shell she had created, were popping to the surface of her being like bubbles on a pot of boiling water. She needed to find a way to settle them so she could focus on something; the ruins, the hawk, her childhood with her mother's stories, this stallion that was able to touch her hardened heart with just a look. Elena's emotions were scattered and spread thin like hay dust thrown to the wind, and she felt as though the pieces could easily flitter away before she could catch them.

Leaning against the "Owl Tree", Elena quietly watched the stallion. His eyes had shifted from that far away gaze to interest in the hay. He had not yet moved toward the food, but she could see his longing and his need. Remaining motionless, she waited, almost holding her breath. Would hunger win over the fear? She shifted her eyes to the ground so the stallion would not feel pushed away. After a time, the sound of released breath and squishing mud indicated that hunger had won. Without moving her body, Elena slowly looked toward the hay pile. The stallion was there, sniffing the hay. Her body was beginning to feel the strain of not moving, but still she remained motionless. A slight breeze ruffled her long dark hair, and a strand tickled her lips and nose. Finally she could stand it no longer; a sneeze erupted, and she reached up to push the wayward strand from her face.

The stallion erupted too. He leaped into the air and ran to the far corner of the pen, nostrils flaring, his breath blowing in loud snorts, his ears straight up and alert, his tail standing out like a flag registering alarm.

Elena sighed, wishing she had been able to stifle the sneeze. Now it would take more time to regain the small amount of trust she had garnered from the stallion that morning. But at least, for those few minutes, her mind had been able to focus and her world had found a tiny amount of order.

Sally smiled looking out the kitchen window as she shredded potatoes for breakfast hash browns. *Amazing*, she thought as she blew a wayward strand of golden red hair out of her eyes. Elena was as still as a statue in the stallion's pen, and yet she exuded more animation in that stillness than at any time since she had been at the ranch. Her whole being seemed to vibrate with new found energy.

Dumping the potatoes into the cast iron fry pan and wiping her hands on a towel hanging from the oven door, Sally turned back to the window. The stallion was spinning around and charging to the corner of his pen. It occurred to Sally that maybe being inside that pen wasn't the safest place for Elena to be. She also knew that a wild horse would normally go well out of their way to stay away from a human. Because Elena seemed far more alive since that stallion had arrived, Sally decided not to press the issue of safety unless she felt it was needed later on. She dropped the eggs onto the skillet, gave the chile a stir, and went to the door to call the family in to eat.

Elena would have gladly forgone the morning meal to stay with the stallion, but she turned to the house at Sally's call. The horse needed to eat too, and chances were he wasn't going to go near that hay again this morning if she stayed. Stepping through the kitchen door, she smiled at Sally, who almost dropped the skillet in surprise. George came through the door just in time to see the encounter and raised his brows at Sally. A smile from that child was a rare occasion and warranted notice.

Was that darned old skinny wild horse all that was required to cause such a change in their sad, serious teenager? George was sure there must be more to it, but no matter the cause, he was downright pleased. Elena even ate more than usual that morning. It almost seemed as though there was another person trapped inside that lithe, strong body, struggling to be known. And there were secrets hiding just behind her eyes. George and Sally were eager to know more about this girl.

Sally briefly locked eyes with her husband, then looked at Elena.

"So. Our new four legged family member is going to need a name, don't you think?"

Without looking up, Elena said, "His name is Hawk." She took another bite of chile-soaked egg and potato.

Sally glanced at her husband and they both smiled. "That's a fine name for him, I think. Nice and short and just seems to fit him."

Elena nodded, her eyes still on her plate. Then she looked up with a puzzled expression.

"Where did he come from?" she asked.

"I picked him up at the sale yesterday," George said. "The

government did another one of their round ups."

She mulled this over for a minute or two, sure there was more to the story. She knew about the government round ups of the wild horses. She knew that a lot of the younger ones would find homes. But Elena also knew that older horses, especially stallions, were considered worthless and a bother and usually went to slaughter.

"Why?" she asked.

Sally couldn't help but snicker a bit under her breath. Lots of people would have asked that question. But not if they knew George the way she did.

Casting his wife a sideways glance that indicated he knew what she was thinking, George chuckled, laughing at himself as he answered.

"There was nobody else to do it."

Elena raised her eyebrows, not understanding their private joke.

"I couldn't see the horse go to slaughter, and there was no where else for him to go. So I bought him and brought him home. Thought he would fit right in."

As George took another bite of his breakfast, Elena sat quietly, considering his statement. *Interesting*, she thought. *Does he really care what happens to an old, wild horse?* Her hardened heart and wounded spirit were having trouble with this concept. She had not trusted any adult in a long time. Instead of continuing the conversation, she averted her eyes and looked out the window.

"May I be excused to go finish my chores?" Elena asked in a controlled voice.

"Of course," said Sally. She had noticed the change in Elena as they talked about the stallion, Hawk. Since that was perhaps the most conversation they had ever had with the girl, she decided to let it go for the time being.

As Elena cleaned what she could of the horse corrals, leaning hard against the wheelbarrow to push it through the mud, her thoughts remained on the Laytons and breakfast. She was feeling confused. While she could not bring herself to trust George and Sally, she felt this place, and her place in it, were different than the other foster homes she had been sent to. Nothing had seemed to connect for her in those other places. Nothing anyone had said had rung true to her. It had all seemed very distant and separate from her.

But no matter what her mind and past experiences told her to think, she couldn't help but feel a connection to something here … to most things here. When she did the barn chores, being with the horses felt right. When the Laytons spoke, something in her wanted to believe them. When she walked on the desert, her feet felt grounded in the sandy soil and the feeling seemed to radiate up her legs and through the rest of her body. *Grounded in a good way*, she thought, smiling to herself.

I need to go back to the mesa, to the ancient village, she was thinking. She had been undecided whether to spend the day with Hawk or to return to the village of her ancestors. Her heart was telling her to go climb the mesa.

Elena finished her morning chores, collected a water bottle and baseball cap to keep her hydrated and shaded from that desert sun, and went in search of Sally.

"I don't think I need your help with anything this morning, Elena," Sally replied to Elena's question. "What are you planning to do with your day?"

"I'd like to go back up the mesa and explore. There are some interesting rocks and things up there." Elena wasn't ready to mention her special place to anyone yet. "I'll be back for lunch."

Sally saw the light in Elena's eyes that had been there yesterday when she had returned home at chore time. *Now what is that girl up to?* she wondered. But all she said was, "I see you have a hat and water bottle. Keep an eye out for snakes and have fun." She watched Elena strike out at a fast clip, as though she had an important appointment.

Something up on that mesa has gotten that girl's attention, she thought. *If we had neighbors I would have sworn she had found herself a boy!* Sally was ninety-nine percent sure that was not the case, though; the ranch was miles from anywhere. So smiling, she shook her head and went in search of her husband.

4

A GHOST IN THEIR WORLD

Elena should have been tired by the time she reached the top of the mesa, but her adrenaline had kicked in with the anticipation of what lay ahead, so she only stopped long enough to catch her breath, get her bearings, and take a few swallows of water before heading out across the mesa top toward her destination. As she walked, she imagined herself running free across the gravely sand on Hawk. She could feel the strength and power of his muscles moving underneath her, carrying her across the mesa almost as though he had sprouted wings. The sound of hooves echoed in the silence of the desert. She could hear the snorts and breaths of the stallion as he ran. Her breathing took on the rhythm of the hoof beats, and she felt as though she could fly! The feeling was so amazing that she was almost disappointed when she reached her special place.

But as she stood, still breathing the rhythm of flight, she brought her mind and spirit back to the earth.

Elena looked around from left to right, wondering which direction to go first. She walked a few steps to a low rock wall that had been the foundation of an ancient building. This room had been round, but only a portion of the foundation was left. Half had crumbled more and had been covered over by blowing sand. A small pinion tree had grown at the base and taken root in the shade of the foundation. Elena sat against the trunk of the tree in the little bit of shade it provided. Comfort and peace washed over her.

Screee, screeee! Elena was awakened by a hawk's cry. But as she looked up to see, she was startled by the fact that she seemed to be in the sky. She felt a floating sensation and a powerful sense of movement that was beginning to be familiar. Wings! *Screeeee!* There it was again. This time she realized it came from her. It was the sound of joy ... and freedom ... ecstasy! *Screeeeee!* She was soaring with the air currents high above the land. There was nothing in her way. Nothing to stop her or slow her down except the limitations of her own winged hawk's body. She felt so strong, so powerful, and so light, floating, soaring. Everything on the landscape far below appeared tiny and inconsequential. She felt the urge to fold her wings and dive. Faster, faster, like a bullet she shot downward, then pulled up just as she reached the ground. Looking down, she was only mildly surprised to see that her hawk talons had turned into horse hooves, and she was again feeling the strength, solidity and fluidity of a horse, running wild and free across the land. Wishing to fly again, she reared up on her hind legs but could not get off the ground. The hooves turned to feet, and she was again a girl, the wild and flowing mane human hair. But the feeling of strength and freedom remained. Her mind stayed open, allowing her soul to wander.

On the mesa at the ancient village, she was surprised to see people. They were going about their business as if they did not see her. Slowly she walked in closer. The ruins were no longer ruins. They were a living village. Since none of the people glanced in her direction, Elena realized she must only be as a ghost in their world.

The people were carrying clay pots full of water and other liquids to cooking fires. There were poles lashed together with strips of bark that appeared to have food drying on them. The buildings were built of rock with wooden beams for support. Soon the buildings began to blur and fade. As she struggled to see, her body began to feel heavy.

"No!" she could feel herself calling silently. "Don't take me back ... I want to stay!" But through the gradually clearing fog, she could see the crumbling foundation of the present-day ruins.

Screee! She heard the hawk call and for a moment held out hope that he would take her back to the ancestors. But she remained grounded in her world, seated under the small pinion tree at the base of the rock foundation.

Elena checked the location of the sun in the sky and was surprised to see that there had been little movement. It was as though her dream had taken no time at all, even though it had taken her hundreds of years from there. The thought set her to wondering about, well, about everything. Standing, she brushed the dirt off her pants and looked around. *Where should I start?* she wondered. Carefully she stepped to the higher side of the foundation, alternately looking at the layout of the location and checking the ground for possible treasures or clues.

Out of the corner of her eye she saw something move. She was sure of it. Standing still and silent, she waited. Breathing shallowly so as not to make a sound, she listened. She heard nothing but the breeze whistling lightly through the rocks and trees and a scrub jay that appeared to be scolding Elena in earnest. In her thoughts she willed the jay to be quiet, but that only seemed to egg him on. She was sure she had seen something move that was not the bird, and there was something in the breeze that chilled her for a moment. Shaken, she stayed still for another minute or two and then decided she must have been imagining things. After all, had she not just dreamed that she had gone hundreds of years back in time and been flying? Elena smiled and continued her exploration.

Soon the sun had moved higher in the sky, and she realized she would need to leave if she were going to make it back for lunch. As she left the site of the ruin heading toward the downhill slope, she felt a hard shove against her back that almost knocked her to the ground. Catching her balance before she fell on a pile of stones and cactus, she swung around to confront her attacker. There was no one there! Heart pounding, she stood still to listen, and just as before heard nothing but wind and the jay scolding her from a tree branch. She was beginning to feel as though something or someone was annoyed by her presence here. This was where she had found memories of her family. This is where she found pieces of history relating to her people. This is where the dreaming had finally found her after such a long absence. There was no way anything was going to keep her from coming back, especially a force that refused to be seen. Again, the warm wind sent a chill through her. She turned and headed down the slope, deep in thought.

5

THE LANGUAGE OF HORSE

Elena was still preoccupied by her morning's adventures as she slipped through the kitchen door just in time for lunch. George had just come in from feeding the cows and was washing up at the kitchen sink while Sally tossed a fresh salad. Looking up from their tasks, both hoped to see the twinkle in Elena's eye that they had seen the day before when she returned from her hike. This time though, consternation and concentration had replaced that twinkle in her eye with a wrinkle in her brow.

With a nod and an effort at a smile, Elena left her cap and water bottle by the door and went to the sink to wash up.

"How was your hike this morning, Elena?" asked Sally.

"It was fine," Elena said. "Wind blowing up on the mesa, as usual."

If Sally was hoping for any clues to Elena's mood, it didn't look as though they would be forthcoming. She looked to George for conversation.

"How is the herd looking, dear?"

"They're holding their own," he replied. "I am going to keep them in the lower field for a while and risk feeding a little more of our hay. Maybe that upper section will green up some from that rain and grow enough grass for winter pasture. At least now the grass that I step on doesn't crunch!" George grinned.

"I know what you mean," said Sally. "My garden is looking much happier. But I feel like I am just growing greens for the wildlife!" She rolled her eyes. "If I fence it off from the deer, the rabbits get it. If I chicken-wire it to keep the rabbits out, the slugs, bugs, and birds get it. It's exasperating, but I guess the wild critters have to eat too. And there's nothing green out there this year except what we water!"

"Well, it just so happens that on my way to the house I noticed the rain sure made your Honeysuckle and Trumpet vines happy. There were a couple of hummingbirds and some bees buzzing around flowers that were trying to open up." George looked pleased with himself as his wife's face lit up.

"Really, George? I had resigned myself to not seeing our little hummers this year. I thought maybe they had found greener pastures."

Elena ate silently. She heard some of the lunch table conversation, but mostly she was deep in thought about her morning. She closed her eyes, trying to bring back the powerful, ecstatic feelings of galloping across the land and flying with the wind. She couldn't bring it back though, not sitting here at the table, so she took another bite of salad and a hard boiled egg.

"Elena," Sally said, "you and I need to make a trip to town soon."

Looking at Sally, Elena wondered why on earth Sally thought she would need to go to town for anything … ever. Town was a place full of gossiping people with prying eyes.

"Why? I don't need anything that I can think of."

Sally shifted in her chair to face the teen.

"Oh yes you do. School starts in a few weeks. You need new clothes and school supplies" She watched expressions fly across the girl's face, from surprise, to horror, to despair.

"Oh, no," said Elena. "I'd forgotten about school." She began fidgeting with her silverware nervously.

Since she had lived in so many different places, Elena had changed schools frequently. She did not make friends easily, so school was a lonely, stressful part of her life. And now she was going to have to ride a bus, with a handful of other kids, 30 miles to the nearest school! Before long she would be going to school in the dark and getting home in the dark. That meant no trips to the mesa village and no time to spend with Hawk except on the weekends.

Despair tore through her at the thought of having to put on hold her newly found, enchanted place on the mesa, and dealing instead with new people and homework.

Sally could empathize with what she suspected Elena was going through. While Sally had only been in one school system her whole life and had seen the same kids from year to year, she had still been different from most of them. Her differences had shaped her friendships and they had been few and far between. Ranch kids were tough due mainly to necessity. Working the land and raising livestock was hard, and most of the kids were not given to expressing much compassion, especially for animals. Like Sally and George, Elena seemed to be firmly connected to the natural world. Sally was sure she was a very sensitive child under her hard protective shell.

"I realize you are not looking forward to the school year, Elena, but the law says you must go. And if you have to go, you might as well have the right supplies and be dressed as the pretty girl you are," Sally said. "I think tomorrow will be a good day to get away, so tonight we can sit down and make a list of what we need to get."

"OK." Elena resigned herself to her fate. "But I don't need much. Please don't waste a lot of money on this."

George smiled. "There won't be any waste, Elena. Don't you worry about it. You work hard here at the ranch. Anything we buy, you have earned. Besides, it might be fun for you and Sally to have a girls' day out."

Elena gave a grimace that was to pass for a smile, and Sally stifled a chuckle.

That girl wants a day in town doing girly stuff about as much as I want ballet slippers, she thought.

After the lunch dishes had been washed, dried, and put away, Elena slipped out the kitchen door and headed for Hawk's pen. He was standing partially shaded by the Owl Tree, his rough, dry red roan coat dappled by sun shining through tree branches and leaves. At first she thought he was dozing in the warm afternoon sun. On closer inspection, she realized the stallion was gazing steadily toward the horizon. After giving Elena a cursory glance, his eyes went back to the horizon. The only movement she could detect in him was the twitching of skin to dislodge a fly. There was a certain intensity to

Hawk's lack of movement, an energy and intensity that Elena had been sharing lately.

I wonder if he's flying like his namesake, she mused, for his whole being was charged with whatever commanded his attention. *Or maybe he's remembering when he was free and ran so fast that he could almost fly.* Even with his emaciated frame and rough, dry hair coat, Hawk had a nobleness about him. Elena closed her eyes and again imagined herself as a horse, running strong and free across the dry, windswept desert, through rock outcroppings, jumping the narrow washes, and charging through the deep sand of the larger ones. Catching her breath, she opened her eyes to see the stallion watching her intently. His eyes were animated and his nostrils fluttered as he softly snorted, his ears turned directly toward her.

"You can feel it too," she breathed, afraid of breaking the spell, the connection between them. Suddenly a rabbit burst out of the sagebrush next to the corral. Both Elena and the stallion jumped, startled from their daydream. After the rabbit had gone, Hawk resumed his watch of the horizon. Elena moved toward the horse. He moved away and began to pace the fence line, slowly walking, back and forth, all the time looking at the horizon.

He wants to fly away home, she sighed. *I have felt that way so many times these past few years.* Tears threatened to fall as she watched the stallion pace back and forth in the small enclosure. *I could release him. Let him run free across the desert and mesas, but his herd is no longer where he can find them.* They were rounded up and sold at auction just as he had been. And there is more food for him right here than anywhere on that drought ridden desert. If he were found running free, this time he would probably be shot.

It was the same for Elena. She could run, but where would she go? It was a long way back home, and there was no one there for her. If the authorities found her, they would just take her away again to another foster home or maybe even the Juvenile Detention since she would be labeled a "runner" in the system. At least here there was a way of life that felt familiar to her. The Layton's appeared to be good people and there was food and a roof over her head. And, of course, Hawk and the village on the mesa.

Leaning against the fence watching Hawk pace, Elena's thoughts returned to her morning at the village. Her exploring that day hadn't yielded a lot of new information, but her dreaming certainly had been interesting. Bits and pieces of early childhood memories began surfacing for her. She could remember sitting at the family meals bored with the adult conversation. She also remembered how she used to shut out the drone of conversation and look into the muted light of the lantern that had hung over the table.

How easy it had been to dream then. Looking into the light, it had always seemed like she had entered a different world. Everything would take on a soft, hazy quality as Elena had entered her own special dream world completely apart from the world she was sitting in at the dinner table. She never got to stay in her special place for very long though. Some adult would notice that her food remained untouched and prompt her to finish eating, pulling her back from her dream.

It seemed she was revisiting that special place whenever she could connect with the natural world here on the high desert. Now that she had found it again, she was in no hurry to give it up by leaving. As she watched Hawk pacing up and down the fence line, his agitation turned her thoughts to her own troubles. School. Shopping. Half hour bus rides morning and night. Now she wanted to start pacing! The confinement that her thoughts were conjuring up was already beginning to take its toll. She could stay still no longer, so she climbed out of the corral and headed for the barn to start setting out hay for the evening feeding.

After doing everything she could to prepare early for her chores, she looked for something new to keep her occupied. *Hawk is unhappy*, she thought. *Nothing here is familiar to him. Surely he misses his herd and feels alone.*

Elena walked back to the stallion's corral and leaned on the fence, deep in thought. To her they seemed as kindred spirits. Both of them in need of belonging. Both of them separated from their families and the lands of their birth where everything had been right.

I wonder if there's a way to help him. She was sure she was feeling his pain in her heart and her gut. That hollow aching feeling of isolation. *If I could somehow learn to speak his language, the language of Horse, we might communicate better.*

Elena thought about what it must be like to live in a herd of horses and how they communicate amongst themselves. *Body language would have to be a priority,* she thought as she slipped through the fence rails and turned to face the horse. He had stopped his pacing and turned his body to face her, his nostrils gently vibrating, taking in her scent. They stood facing each other, horse and girl, neither of them moving a foot or leg, but locked in eye contact.

So he listens carefully, thought Elena as she saw the stallion's ears turned directly toward her. *And he smells me.*

Keeping her gaze locked on his, Elena took a step forward. Hawk snorted and stepped back, trembling, his muscles tense with readiness. Elena stopped, took a deep breath, and slowly released it, trying to release her own tension with that breath. She wanted Hawk to relax.

Maybe if I seem to take my attention away from him somehow, he won't feel so threatened. I know when a stranger stares at me it makes me really uncomfortable. She lowered her gaze to his shoulder where she would still be able to sneak a peak at his face so that she might read his intention. As she did this, she could feel an ever so slight change in his countenance. He released a quiet breath that sounded like a sigh. Still looking at Hawk's shoulder, she took another step forward while taking another deep breath and slowly releasing it.

Her heart gave a jump when she saw him stand his ground. Elena stopped and slowly raised her gaze to his. He was watching her intently and quivering with anticipation, but holding his ground. In her mind, Elena stopped all thought of forward motion and again breathed into her intention. A small amount of tension appeared to drain from the stallion as he released another breath. They stood this way for a minute or so, just looking at each other. Elena lowered her gaze to his shoulder again, and he appeared to relax a little more, so she decided to try something more.

This time she turned her gaze toward Hawk's hindquarters. She saw him tense in readiness and she took a slow, small step in the direction of her gaze. It was as though she had given him a little push, and he stepped forward, away from her. She stopped, and after a few steps so did he. When she slowly lifted her gaze to again meet his, he was watching and listening with his ears still cocked directly toward her and turned his body to again face her.

A small smile came to Elena as she realized that bits and pieces of Hawk's language were beginning to take form for her. She shivered slightly with the anticipation of being able to communicate with this four-legged brother.

"Elena!" A voice called her up from her concentration. "Elena! Dinner in half an hour!" Sally called out. "Better get after the chores!"

Wow, thought Elena, *time really flies! It's a good thing I have the feed mixed and ready to put out and the pens cleaned.*

She sighed, wishing she didn't have to stop now that she was on the path of discovering the new world of communication with her friend. Turning her back to the stallion, she took a couple of steps toward the fence, then looked back over her shoulder. Hawk was still watching her. In a few more steps she had reached the fence and shuffling sounds made her stop. Elena lowered her gaze first to the ground, then slowly turned her head. The stallion had taken a step in her direction, had stopped, and was watching. She sent Hawk a silent salutation and a smile, then left to get his supper.

6

TOMORROW

Elena had a hard time going to sleep. Tomorrow was the trip to town, and she did not want to go. Since there were only a few weeks of freedom left to her, she surely did not want to waste any time on something that would take her away from Hawk and her adventures on the mesa. And the Laytons acted like she should be excited about the prospect of shopping.

Yuck! she fumed silently. *Stores and people and their questioning stares.* Strangers always pretended to be well-meaning when all they really wanted, in Elena's opinion, was fuel for their gossip mill. Small towns rarely had anything or anyone new to talk about, so she would be fair game for quite a while. Groaning, she pushed her pillows higher so she could sit against them and then punched them in frustration.

Going to town with Sally wouldn't be the worst part, though. Riding the bus to school. That would be hell. On the bus there would be no one to run interference between the clannish group of kids that had been riding that bus together since they started school and Elena, the new girl. The bus driver would be too busy to notice and probably wouldn't care anyway. A single tear slid down her cheek at the thought of being the new kid. Again. She squirmed against her pillows and wiped the errant tear from her cheek in anger. She wouldn't let them make her cry! No!

Whoo hoo, whoo hoo. The owl was in the tree outside Elena's window. She stopped her fidgeting and fuming to listen. *Whoo hoo, whoo hoo.* Elena let the sound take her away from her pain for a moment. The Owl, her mother had told her, was wise. The Owl could see in the night and could turn its head to see all directions.

"Learn to see things with the eyes of an owl, Elena. Look closely at everything before you make up your mind about anything." Elena smiled at her mother's words. She could almost see her mother sitting across from her, holding her hands and looking into her eyes. As her thoughts wandered in the past, sleep crept in with the owl's lullaby.

Whoo hoo, whoo hoo, whoo hoo.

***

"If we don't get more rain soon, we're going to have to sell the calves early." George stared out at the night sky studded with stars and a waxing moon, then looked at his wife. "We'll have to sell the calves to buy more hay to winter the cows."

George spoke in a soft voice and appeared calm, but Sally knew better. She could see the furrow in his brow under the tan line from his hat. This could well be their last chance to hang on to the cattle. Many of their neighbors were having to sell out, the drought wasn't easing up, and the hay prices were going up again. Selling the calves early meant that they would have to go through the sale barn. Most of the buyers there were buying for the feedlots. George and Sally would do all they could to keep their calves from going through the stress of the sale ring and the toxic feed practices of most feedlots. If they could somehow afford to winter the calves, they could take them straight to the processor from the mesa they had been born on. It was easier and kinder for the calves. The resulting meat would be healthier too, since their cattle only ate the good native high desert grass and whatever hay was needed to supplement it. They needed rain now!

"At least the market is staying up," she said. "If we have to sell, at least we have a good chance of getting a fair price. Not like last year when the market dropped by almost half!"

They sat in silence on the creaky old porch swing, both lost in thought for a few minutes. George put his arm across Sally's shoulders, admiring her soft profile in the moonlight. A slight breeze gently lifted the curls in her hair and he sighed, thinking how much she still looked like the high school girl he had fallen in love with decades ago.

"You and Elena are headed to town tomorrow?"

"I thought we would go right after breakfast," Sally said. "It will probably take most of the day. That girl doesn't have much to wear, and what she does have isn't suitable for anything but ranch work. I'm sure she would rather climb rocks and shovel manure than dress like a young lady and go to school."

"She seems to be settling in a little," George said. "Do you think she might eventually like it here? Maybe she will stay and not take off like they said she did from the other foster home. She seems to really like the horses, especially that skinny ole stallion."

Sally rolled her eyes and smiled.

"Yes, that skinny old stallion. Hawk. Who would have thought that he would be so much help? It will be worth the cost of his feed if he can break through her defenses. He seems to be her best friend at the moment. Although I am wondering if there isn't something or someone else. She takes off lickety split to that mesa every chance she gets!"

George rubbed his head. "She's sure all fired up when she comes back from there. What do you think she's doing up there?"

"I sure don't know," said Sally as she gazed out across the moonlit pasture. "Elena is seventeen, and if we lived anywhere else I'd say she had found herself a boy. But there are none within miles from here and she hasn't been anywhere to meet anyone, so it must be something else. I'm sure the hike up to the top takes the edge off her emotions and gives her some time to think. Maybe that's at least part of it. For now I don't see any reason to not let her go. As long as she's not giving us reason to mistrust her, I think it might be wise to give her as much freedom as possible. School starts soon enough, and I am guessing it won't be an easy time for any of us."

George had a quick flashback to his days in high school and grimaced.

"Nope. That bunch in town won't make it easy on her, Ill bet." His gray eyes were dancing and the corner of his mouth twitched as he said, "We made it through in pretty good shape, though."

Sally gave him a peck on the cheek.

"Yes we did, dear. I wouldn't change a thing."

Smiling, she changed the subject.

"The horses are out of grain, so I'll be going to the feed store. And, of course, we need groceries." Sally grinned at George. "Think you can fend for yourself at lunchtime?"

"There's always PB&J," George said. "What more could a guy need?"

Smiling, they sat, comfortable and content in each other's company, the swing gently rocking them toward sleep.

7

DREAMING THE HERD

Elena slipped out of her bed before the sun could peek over the horizon. She wanted to get an early start so she would have a little time with Hawk before she and Sally left for town. She slipped on her jeans, a T-shirt, and a sweatshirt. It always seemed chilly just before the sun came up. On this high desert, the temperatures often fluctuated forty or fifty degrees between night and day, so layers of clothing were called for.

She made her bed and tip-toed down the stairs. As Elena's eyes adjusted to the predawn light, she grabbed a banana from the kitchen counter, pulled her vest from the wall hook, and shoved her feet into her rubber chore boots. The cool air felt soft and velvety on her face as she slipped out the door and down the steps. She stopped to listen to the early morning sounds. The birds were just beginning to stir and chirp the tiniest bit. There was an occasional snort from a horse and shuffle of a hoof. She jumped a little and grinned as a hummingbird shot past her on its way to look for the morning blossoms that would be on the verge of opening. Those hummers were early risers.

On her way to the barn, she made a quiet detour to the stallion pen to see what Hawk was up to. She could see his silhouette backlit by the predawn sky. He was standing quietly, but his head was up and he appeared to still be gazing at that horizon.

As she stood watching the horse, Elena had the oddest feeling that someone was watching her. Her first thought was that maybe George had risen early as well and was watching her from the porch. As she turned to look, a flurry of commotion broke loose in the Owl Tree next to Hawk. It startled Elena, and she jerked back around to see the owl rousing herself from her nighttime hunting perch in the tree and heading for wherever it was that she spent the days resting.

Geez. Her heart was pounding a mile a minute! Hawk, however, appeared completely undisturbed. He had already grown used to Owl's coming and going. *Maybe I will sleep out here sometime and see what goes on at night,* she thought.

She fed the four ranch horses and spent a little time with each of them, as she had started doing before Hawk arrived. She ran her fingers through the long mane hairs, talking to each horse as she combed.

"It's been a while, hasn't it?" As she spoke softly to Junior, George's stout bay Quarter Horse, he turned his head slightly from his feed bucket as though to hear her better. Little bits of grain dribbled from the corner of his mouth as he munched contentedly. His ears twitched back and forth with the sound of her voice. She gave him a good rub on his chest and moved on to the next horse. *It's so peaceful out here,* she thought. *I feel like one of the herd.* She stayed with them until they had finished their grain and started on the hay. Giving the last horse a final pat, she carried the feed buckets back to the barn.

The sun began to peak over the horizon as Elena headed back to Hawk's pen. Before it was even fully risen she could feel the heat. Every bit of moisture from the rain a couple of days earlier had dried up, and each time her boot came in contact with the ground, a puff of powdery, dry dust billowed up. She peeled off her vest and sweatshirt as she walked. Another hot, dry day ahead.

The stallion snorted and rumbled a little, low in his throat, anticipating his breakfast as she approached. When she stepped inside the enclosure, he backed away, watching her every move. She set the bucket, containing his small ration of grain on the ground between them and stepped back a few paces. Hawk stood watching, waiting for her to leave the pen. This time she stood her ground, quiet, immobile, looking at the ground instead of at the horse.

They stood this way, no movement, no sound, except for the air moving in and out of their lungs and the quiet early morning song of the birds. But there was a tension, a throbbing energy between them so strong it resembled a heartbeat. Elena focused on her breathing as she stared at the ground. A picture began to form in her mind. Misty, dreamlike, an outline took form and then became animated. As the mist began to clear, a herd of horses ran free across the desert, snorting, hooves hammering. Then, like a flash of lightning, it was gone. She heard Hawk snort.

The whole sequence happened so quickly it left her breathless. It was all she could do to stay still and not jerk her head up to look at Hawk. Slowly she allowed her gaze to move to the stallion. He was staring intently at her, and she felt as though she was falling into those dark brown eyes, as though she was being drawn into his dream. Had he been dreaming the herd too? Was it his herd? She was still trying to separate herself from the vision when Hawk shook his head and snorted, breaking the connection between them. She felt it and stepped back one pace. She was surprised to see him step forward after a few seconds and drop his head into the feed bucket. He snatched up one quick mouthful of the grain, jerked his head up, and wheeled around, creating distance between them once again.

Elena wasn't disappointed, she was excited! Even though she longed to comb her fingers through his thick, black tangled mane, she was well aware with a wild horse that might never happen. This was progress. A horse's main source of protection was flight. To stick his head down in a bucket, which limited his vision severely, with a human present, this was definitely progress. Hawk's need for food was able to override his flight instinct, so maybe there was the tiniest bit of trust forming. Smiling, she stepped out of the pen to pick up the hay she had left by the gate. She put the hay near the grain bucket, checked the water in the tank, and sighed as she heard the kitchen door open and close. The fun was over. Today was town day.

8

TOWN

An hour later Elena had changed into a clean pair of jeans, a T-shirt, and sneakers.

A breakfast of lean steak, fresh eggs, and green chile had been eaten, the breakfast dishes done, and 3 PB&J sandwiches made and stored for George's lunch. Sally and Elena got in the ranch truck, waved good bye to George, and headed on down the dusty gravely ranch road toward the old two lane highway that led to town. There was nothing to see between the ranch and the highway except cow pastures, cows, jackrabbits, and herds of antelope.

You had to watch carefully. Those antelope crawled through the fences to get in the road. There was a little bit of green growing in the bar ditches that they liked to feed on, and the antelope weren't very street-smart. Often they would run right down the middle of the road in front of the truck. It was usually best to stop and wait for them to find a place to crawl back through the fences into the pastures.

As they crossed the cattle guard and turned onto the highway, Sally glanced over at Elena. The girl seemed absorbed in the scenery, so she didn't bother her with questions or conversation. They were comfortable enough with the silence, and there would be plenty of time for talk. The drive to town took over an hour. Sally liked the drive, even when she was alone. Especially when she was alone. It gave her time to think. She felt like her imagination worked best out there where no one expected anything from her except to stay between the lines. She pulled a CD out of its case and fed it to the player.

Elena also liked being on the road. She watched the tops of the power poles for red tail hawks. They liked to hunt from those high places where they could see forever. She also like to keep an eye out when they passed a pasture that had a dirt stock tank. These were like ponds that the ranchers built into the ground to catch rainwater for watering the livestock. You never knew what you might see out there if there had been a recent rain. Sally had told her stories of pairs of beautiful white snowy egrets that had spent the night on the fence of the corral at the ranch on their way to the wetlands southwest of there. There could be ducks, herons, and even an occasional osprey. Elena was hoping they would get the monsoon rains this summer. Not just for the grass and trees, but because she wanted to see all of these water birds that seemed so exotic to her and so out of place on that dry, dusty desert.

After a while, Sally slowed the truck to cross a set of railroad tracks. Just as she started to accelerate, she suddenly braked, pulled the truck to the side of the road, and pointed to the tops of some old trees.

"Look Elena, an eagle!"

Elena quickly put the window down and stuck her head out. Sure enough, there in the top branches of the gnarly, almost leafless old tree was a huge Golden Eagle. Her heart was doing flips and her face was flush with excitement. Eagles were powerful medicine. They were sacred, and their feathers revered by her people and used in sacred ceremony.

"Eagle brings one closer to Spirit. Eagle flies close to the sun, Elena." It was her mother's voice again.

Elena wanted to jump out of the truck and get closer, but she knew that would probably send the great bird away.

Sally had turned the truck off and was content to wait until Elena was ready. She smiled to herself, thinking of the things that got that girl excited. The things that made her smile; the things that brought life to her eyes. She realized that many of the things that excited Elena also brought added joy to her and to George. There were days when she was out walking that the earth seemed to beckon to her and she felt like dropping to the ground and rolling in the dirt just for the sheer joy of it. Those were the kind of feelings that had set her apart from most of the other kids when she was in school. When they had spare time, they either wanted to rip roar around on four wheelers, or go out with guns and shoot things, or sit in front of the TV when their folks allowed it. Sally had never liked all of the noise and violence attached to those forms of entertainment and had preferred instead to sit in a tree watching for birds and wildlife or walking up the rock-lined washes keeping an eye out for treasures that washed down from the mesa. Beautiful stones with fossils of shells, bits of old pottery, an occasional arrowhead.

Arrowheads! Pottery! It was like someone had just switched on a light bulb in her dusty old brain, thought Sally. Of course. That was what had drawn Elena to the mesa. It was the old ruins. She looked thoughtfully at the girl in the passenger seat still completely absorbed in the eagle.

Well, that's a relief, Sally chuckled to herself. At least now we can be pretty sure what the attraction is up there.

"I think we had better get going," she said. "We have a lot to do in town and feed to unload when we get home. George is repairing fences today, and he isn't going to want to deal with feed."

Elena reluctantly pulled her head back inside and put the window up.

As they traveled North, more houses and barns appeared. They marveled at the green of the irrigated hay fields. Such a contrast to the neighboring desert pastures that didn't have water. Soon town became visible on the horizon.

"Let's get your school clothes and supplies first, Elena. Then we can find some lunch."

Sally pulled into the Walmart parking lot. She really disliked shopping there, it was so impersonal and had been the death of several local businesses, but there weren't many options unless they went another forty miles to the city. They could get all the school supplies and most of the clothing Elena would need right there and save time.

Elena looked around the women's clothing section and shook her head. Walking a little farther she saw what she was looking for and headed to the men's clothing and the blue jeans. Sally smiled. *Of course,* she thought, *what else would she have expected?*

"I only need a couple pairs of jeans," said Elena. "And maybe a T-shirt."

"Oh no you don't," Sally laughed. "Winter will come sooner or later, with or without snow, and you are going to need some warm clothes. And some nice shirts and sweaters for Fall. Surely you can find something here that you like."

Elena looked around and finally settled for some cotton and flannel shirts, a couple of sweaters, and a fleece jacket. She already had a good warm vest. Sally picked up a couple of pairs of jeans for herself and for George. They always needed more work clothes.

"We can get boots or shoes at the feed store, Elena. And they will be much nicer and last longer than anything we could find here. Let's grab some school supplies and get out of this place."

They paid the cashier and loaded the bags in the truck.

"It isn't really time for lunch. Where are we going next?" Elena asked quietly.

This was the first conversation Elena initiated all day, thought Sally.

"Where would you like to go?"

"Is there a bookstore in town? I'd really like to get something to read."

"Yes, there is a bookstore. And I love to read too, so lets go check it out."

You don't have to talk me into it, thought Sally as she pulled the truck out of the huge, half empty parking lot. *I could spend all day in a bookstore. When you live as far away from everything as we do, books become excellent friends, and great reminders that there is still a whole world beyond the ranch. And just where did they think all the traffic would come from to fill that parking lot way out here? That Walmart parking lot was always more than half-empty.* She turned back onto Main Street and headed for the bookstore in the older, more familiar part of town.

***

Walking through the front door of the bookstore, Sally said, "Elena, I will meet you at the checkout in half an hour. Treat yourself to two or three good books. We may not get back to this store for a while." Then she headed off to the gardening section.

Elena looked around a bit, familiarizing herself with the store while deciding what type of books to get. She didn't remember ever getting to choose her own books. Mostly she had just read whatever books her foster families already had. When she was younger, her parents had picked out books at second hand stores or books had been given to them. She wanted to make sure that she got the most out of this visit and went first to the section that was all about New Mexico.

I could spend a half a day right here, she thought. She pulled a book off the shelf that was full of old stories about the area and flipped through it. Then she found one with photos of old pottery and other artifacts with information about old historic places in New Mexico. Tucking that book under her arm, she moved on to the animal section to look for books about horses. She flipped through several, written by different trainers. None of them looked as though they would be helpful in dealing with a wild stallion fresh off the range, so she didn't make a selection there. After that, she looked in the fiction section for a good story. It didn't take her long to pick out two more books, being careful to not pick expensive ones. She didn't feel right about Sally paying for them.

On her way to the checkout, she passed the art and photography section. There were large photography books out on a center table, and one of them caught her eye. She picked it up, flipped through it and stopped at one of the photos. She gazed at it for a moment, then turned around, put the other books back where she had found them, and continued on to the front of the store with just the one large book. She met Sally back at the checkout counter, smiling excitedly and shyly at the same time.

Sally looked surprised at Elena's selection. *Just one large book,* she thought. *And a photographic art book at that. Learning more about this girl every day.* Smiling, she noted without surprise that the photos were of horses.

"Did you find what you wanted, Elena?" asked Sally. "I had a hard time deciding! There were so many good books to choose from."

Elena nodded, her eyes shining. She was already trying to think of a way to earn some money for the next book-buying adventure.

"I hope we can come back here sometime soon," she said.

"I could spend hours in here," Sally said as she paid the cashier and picked up the heavy bag full of books. "Well, I don't know about you, but I feel hungry enough to eat a whole cow."

As Elena followed her out of the store, she realized she was pretty hungry too. They put their purchases in the truck and then walked up the block to the Cafe.

The temperature outside was in the nineties, and after drinking a pitcher of water between them, they realized that they weren't as hungry as they were thirsty. So they split a large salad and decided on an appetizer to share. Then they started on another pitcher of water.

"You know, you can have more to eat if you are still hungry, Elena," Sally said as she eyed Elena's empty plate. "Would you like some dessert?"

Elena shook her head. "Oh, no, thanks. Really, that was just right. The salad was huge and the fried zucchini great." What she didn't tell Sally was how excited she was. Elena could not remember ever having so many new things, just for her.

"Two more stops then," Sally said as she put money on the table and stood up. "Off to the feed store, then groceries and back to the ranch."

Sally pulled into the dirt parking lot of the feed store and backed the truck up to the warehouse loading dock. She had to stretch her back and neck to see behind her.

"Being short sure has its drawbacks," she mumbled. "OK, Elena. Why don't you go on in and start looking at the boots? I'll order the feed and be right behind you."

Elena's eyes widened as she stepped through the door. The place was huge! And it looked like they stocked everything you could think of that pertained to ranching, farming, gardening, and livestock. This *is way better than Walmart,* she thought, smiling. She checked the signs hanging at the end of each aisle and found the clothing and footware section.

Wow! A whole aisle dedicated to just women's boots. This might be tougher than she thought. So much to choose from. She walked the aisle first to see what was there and realized that there was a section for work boots and hiking boots, and there was also a section for fashion boots and shoes. She snorted and rolled her eyes at the latter. What on earth would she ever do with a pair of pink, pointy-toed boots? Or bright blue with black and gold stitching?

She went back to the work boot section and looked for her size. She narrowed the choice down to half a dozen styles. Thoughtfully, she picked each one up and looked at the soles to see if they would hold up under ranch work and still be comfortable for school. The reminder of school made her grimace. There was not a lot of difference in the soles. Now she paid more attention to the uppers. One pair had suede uppers. They went to the bottom of the list. Suede was hard to clean and didn't usually hold up as well as heavier leather. The other pairs had good leather uppers. She had narrowed her choice down to three pairs. Then she picked up the last boot and let out a sigh. This boot had good heavy leather, but at the same time it was soft and supple. It was a beautiful mahogany color, and she could barely take her hands and eyes off of it.

Guess I should try them on, she thought. She took a boot from the box marked with her size, 7 ½, and slipped it on. Oh, it felt like heaven. She pulled the other one on and stepped in front of the mirror. They were truly beautiful and incredibly comfortable.

"Did you find a pair you like?" Sally asked. She had come around the corner while Elena was looking at the boots in the mirror.

"These are the only ones I've tried on, but I love them, and they fit really well," Elena said as she took the boots off and returned them to the box.

Sally glanced around at the other boots displayed on the shelves.

"Are you sure you wouldn't like something dressier?"

"Oh no. These are perfect. And tough enough that I can wear them to work in next year too." Elena said, surprising herself to be even thinking about the next year and still being at the ranch.

Sally also noticed the implication in Elena's reply, and it pleased her.

"The feed is all loaded. Bring your boots. Let's pay, get groceries, and head home."

9

THUNDERHEADS TO THE EAST

George stepped out the kitchen door and stood on the back steps. He pushed his hat back so that he could wipe the sweat off his forehead with his shirt sleeve. *Geez, this is a hot day to be out building fence. It's a never-ending job. If my own cows weren't going through the wire, the neighbor cows were. They were all looking for food and thought nothing of pushing down a fence to get into the next pasture.*

He had just gotten home and gone in the house to wash up some and have that last PBJ sandwich that he had saved from lunch, knowing from experience that a snack would come in handy after an afternoon like this one.

The girls should be home pretty soon, he thought. *Sure am glad I didn't have to go shop. A huge burger at the Cafe definitely would have been good, though.* He smiled and, out of habit, glanced up at the horizon to the West, over the mesa. All the ranchers did that several times a day, looking, hoping, to see storm clouds. If the weather forecaster from Albuquerque mentioned rain anywhere in the state, doors opened all over ranch country as the ranchers stepped out to see if maybe they were going to be blessed with precipitation. It was not unusual to be able to stand in one's sunny, dry yard and watch it rain on the neighbor's pasture, or to have most of the top soil blown away at your place while a sheet of water from a major thunderstorm drenched the mesa.

Nothing to the West but bright blue sky and bright sunlight. *That figures,* thought George. But his heart sped up a bit as he looked to the East. There were some thunderheads forming up there. *That could mean most anything. Might mean high winds, or dry lightning and flash floods. Maybe though, just maybe, it might mean rain.* He stepped down and started across the yard to the stallion pen. The horse, Hawk, had his head up, his nose pointing East and his nostrils flared. He was sniffing for something, was it moisture? *Could that old horse smell moisture coming in?* George felt more hope. Horses were good at that, smelling things that humans couldn't. In the wild, their lives often depended on that sense of smell. It warned them of intruders, it led them to food, and it led them to water.

Hawk had stopped sniffing the air and was looking at George.

"Well, old boy. Things are a little bit different for you now than the first time we met. It hasn't been so long, just a couple of days, but I do believe you are beginning to put a little meat on those old bones." George leaned on the fence and met the stallion's gaze.

Hawk snorted and tossed his head, but he didn't move away.

"I know it isn't the same as running with your herd," continued George, "but it's going to have to do for now. Maybe Elena can give you enough company to tide you over."

The stallion snorted again, and George smiled at the light in the horse's eyes. The old boy was definitely coming to life.

"I sure hope you can tolerate civilization when you start feeling good again, because it's going to be the only chance you have."

George turned away from the horse to listen. Sure enough, he heard the sound of a vehicle in the distance, and it sounded like the diesel engine of the ranch truck. He smiled and headed for the driveway. From there he could see the tell-tale dust swirling up from the road, indicating that there was a vehicle about to come over the hill. He walked to the barn and opened the large double doors so Sally could back the truck in when she arrived.

10

LIVING IN THE HUMAN WORLD

Elena enjoyed the drive back to the ranch. It had occurred to her that nobody had really paid much attention to her in town. She liked that. After having worried so much about being under scrutiny as the new girl in town, she was pleased that her worries were unfounded. They had not run into anyone that Sally knew well. There had been a few stares, but that was to be expected and didn't really bother her too much.

Shopping for school supplies and clothes were necessary evils and had been dispensed with in a practical manner. But the bookstore, that had been the highlight of the day for her. The bookstore! Being there was like being in a dream world. She could have spent hours there investigating the different sections. Even though the store was small compared to the big chain stores, they still had a large selection. The history and anthropology books about New Mexico had sucked her right in. She would have gladly sat right there and read them all. Especially the ones about indigenous cultures, past and present. Books with information about the old ruins around the state. The ones that told the stories of the old cultures really captured her attention. As she had read little bits of them while standing at the bookshelves, she could envision the mesa ruins and the treasures that were hidden there.

She had moved to the Animal section. What she had really

needed was a book with information about working with wild horses. She needed something practical that would help her, help Hawk survive in a world of humans.

The typical training book would be of no help to her at this stage of the game. What she needed was something that could help her connect to a wild animal that had spent his whole life as a herd animal. She needed to be able to convince him that the human world could be worth living in. That was an interesting concept, she thought, since she was still trying to convince herself of the same thing!

Finding that book had not proven to be a simple matter. She had found books about training for the different disciplines and breeds in the show ring. She had found books about starting colts and others about equipment. There were books for beginners about how to groom a horse and saddle it. There were also books about horse keeping and feeding and building barns. She had gotten frustrated then, because she was running out of time. She had been even more frustrated when she ran into books that talked about something called "Natural Horsemanship" but seemed to be more about special gimmicks and specialized equipment than anything practical.

Geez, she had thought. *I don't remember it being this complicated when I was growing up.* When she was little, her father had let her watch when he worked with some of the wild horses that were rounded up on the reservation. He had not had special halters or sticks with strange things tied on them. But he had a lot of patience, and he also had seemed to have a feel for how the horse would react to things. It had seemed more intuitive and practical than just an assembly-line training program.

Elena had glanced around and had noticed a sale table in the center aisle. There were large photographic books that some people called "coffee table" books.

Her eyes had landed on two. In the first one, the photographer had concentrated on horse herds in action, some in the mountains, others on the plains. The other book focused on close-ups of these powerful creatures full of natural grace. There were photos that zoomed in on the eyes, intense with wildness and lit with the fire of freedom. Still other photos concentrated on muscles in different parts of the body. The way the photographer had used the light in these photos made the power and movement stand out with grace and beauty. *What a wonderful talent that photographer had,* thought Elena. *To be able to translate so much of those living, wild beings into print for the world to see.*

Glancing at the clock, Elena had realized that Sally would soon be waiting for her at the check out. She then made a decision and had gone back to the beautiful photographic art book with the close-ups of the horses and looked at the price. Even on sale, it was about the same as two or three of the other books put together. If she put the book about the ruins back, she wouldn't feel so bad about getting this one. So she had put it back, making a mental note of the title and where it was located so she could find it easily the next time. Thinking about having had to leave that book behind caused her to let out a deep sigh.

Sally glanced at her. "Is everything OK, Elena?" she asked as she put the windows up and turned on the air conditioning. Late afternoon in July on the desert was about as hot as things could get without the monsoon rains to cool the air. The girl smiled and nodded.

"We might as well get a little pampering," Sally said. "It's gonna be a hot, sweaty job unloading those fifty pound bags of feed. But it sure will be a good feeling to have that feed room full again for a little while. And the horses will appreciate it too!"

Elena chuckled at the last remark.

"They sure enjoy their grain," she said. "Especially Junior. It always looks like he's rolling it around in his mouth and sucking on it to get the last bit of flavor!"

Sally laughed.

"He has always done that too," she said. "We used to think his teeth were bad or something, so we had the vet check them. But they were fine. I think you are right, he is just getting the most out of his favorite time of day."

Elena got caught up in watching the passing scenery. The late afternoon light cast a lot of shadows, but where the light was hitting it had an intense quality to it that made the contrast exceptionally beautiful. The mesas seemed to stand out from the horizon as though in a 3-D movie, and every craggy rock face seemed sculpted and full of character.

As the sun began to move more toward the western horizon, the blue of the sky became so intense it looked almost unreal against the bright reds and browns and greens of the mesas. In a few hours the sky would begin to stripe with the purples, mauves, oranges, reds, and golds of sunset.

The eastern sky was an entirely different story, however. Thunderclouds had been building all afternoon. Huge clouds, white and yellow in the billowy towers that were quickly multiplying at the top and almost black at the bottom, creating dark shadows across the flat pastureland to the East. The thunderheads were sending down jagged threads of lightning all across the horizon. The Eastern Plains of New Mexico often receive violent storms full of electricity and extremely high winds. These storms usually did not extend far enough West to hit the area where the Laytons lived, but they certainly provided interesting entertainment in the form of light shows. And every once in a while, they provided moisture from the western edge of the storm.

This was almost like being in two worlds at once. A storm building in the East, and the incredible light and blue sky to the West. Elena watched a red tail hawk circling lazily and majestically above them, and the sight took her back to the evenings of her childhood.

"Bring more wood for the fire," her mother would be saying. "I have bread baking." She could picture her mother standing on the porch wiping the sweat off of her face. They had only the wood stove and the outdoor oven to cook on in those days. Her mother had been baking bread that way since she had been a child learning from her own mother. Sometimes the heat would be almost unbearable in the summertime, but her mother had always had a full meal on the table when it was time to eat.

Her father had been a good provider and brought home wild game.

They had such things as rabbit or venison stew, elk steaks, and wild turkey as the mainstay of their meals.

Sally glanced at Elena and wondered at the dreamy, far-away look in her eyes.

Teenagers! she thought. *You never know what they are thinking. I'm not so old that I can't remember that age and the dreams I had. Someday I hope Elena will talk about her dreams.*

10

MONSOON JOY

Sally put on the turn signal and turned onto the ranch road. As she did, a great big splat hit the windshield. At first she thought it was a bug. But then another splash hit, and another. They were raindrops. She and Elena looked at each other with barely controlled glee and started laughing. Rain!

"Uh oh," Sally said. "We had better move it along. We have all of those bags of feed in the back." But she didn't look terribly concerned. She still had a big smile plastered across her face as she stepped harder on the accelerator.

They pulled into the ranch driveway a few minutes later, and busted out laughing again. George was standing in the driveway by the barn, his hat off and head tipped back, mouth open in a huge smile, letting the light rain wash his face. Little rivulets of water were running down his cheeks tracing tracks in the dirt and sweat.

Sally quickly turned the truck around and backed into the barn so that the feed would not get ruined. She shut the truck off, jumped out, ran to her husband, and gave him a huge hug. Elena opened the tailgate of the truck and started unloading sacks of feed. George and Sally, now good and damp from the rain shower, hurried to help. Marveling at the strength in that lean teenage body, they both tried to remember the feeling of being a strong, young teen. But it had been too long. While they might remember what their thoughts and dreams had been at that age, their bodies were a different story.

With the three of them working, it did not take long to unload the 20 bags of feed. They emptied what would fit into the grain bin and stacked the rest on wooden pallets to keep them off the floor.

CRASH! All three of them jumped, startled at the close lightning hit. They went to the door of the barn, pulling one of the big double doors closed, but leaving the other open so they could watch the storm.

The wind had picked up, blowing the branches of the trees so that they whipped back and forth wildly. The horses were all huddled together, their tails to the storm, heads down. The sky was so dark it looked like dusk except to the West, where there was still a line of blue low to the horizon and sunshine on the mesa. The sunlight filtering through the rain created an incredible double rainbow.

The squall only lasted about twenty minutes. The bulk of the storm moved farther East toward Texas leaving cool air and rain soaked ground that smelled like life. Living earth. Breathing, dying, and composting life.

George, Sally, and Elena still stood in the barn doorway breathing in the fresh, rain-washed air, and watching the dissipating rainbow. Steam was rolling off the warm ground, and the sun reclaimed the sky as though the storm had never been.

A monsoon! George and Sally felt giddy and grabbing each other, danced a jig in the nearest mud puddle. Elena watched them in disbelief. She had never seen adults act that way before. Then a smile took over her face, and tears almost welled up before she could stop them. She was overwhelmed by an unfamiliar feeling. It wasn't a bad feeling, not sadness or anger. It was almost mysterious, this thing that started in the pit of her stomach and worked it's way up through her heart and pressed against her tear ducts. It was as though the heaviness she had carried around for so long was fighting to get out.

Since she didn't understand it, she did her best to quell the feeling, but it wouldn't go completely away.

Embarrassed, she mumbled something about starting the chores and walked back into the barn to prepare the evening feed. It wouldn't take long tonight. The water tanks would all be overflowing from the gutters still running with water from the roofs. *Going to be a muddy mess, though,* she thought.

Sally pulled the truck from the barn to the house, and she and George, amidst giggles and jokes, unloaded the groceries while Elena took care of the horses. As usual, she fed Hawk last, so if there was time left before dinner she could spend it with him.

Tonight Hawk looked like a drowned rat. He was sopping wet, his mane and tail hanging like big hunks of the Spanish moss that hung in some of the trees. He had also rolled since the rain and patches of him looked like wet adobe. Since his roan coat was wet and matted down, she could count his ribs. But he no longer looked like death. His hide was beginning to look more alive, filled out, hydrated like the earth after a rain. Weight gain was just a matter of time and patience, but it would come.

Hawk didn't seem to mind being a walking mud bog. He really seemed quite pleased with himself. Looking at her through the long damp forelock hair that hung down his face almost to his nostrils, he shook his head, sending water flying all around, and then snorted. Elena laughed as she carried his grain bucket in and set it down between them. He looked at her again and then stomped his foot, sending mud flying everywhere. Elena did not respond except to smile at him, so he stomped again.

"Horse," Elena said, "I am going to have to strip down to my underwear before Sally will let me into the house if you don't quit throwing mud on me."

She stood her ground, and he stood his. But not for very long. She finally averted her gaze from him to the bucket. He waited, watching, for another minute or so and then stepped up to get his grain. Snatching a mouthful, he jerked his head up out of the bucket quickly so that he could watch her, but he only stepped back a couple of steps.

The sun was dropping faster toward the mesa top, and it was almost dusk. The smell of dinner cooking floated out the back door and teased her senses. She went back to the gate to get the pile of hay she had left there. She turned to carry it to one of the dryer places under the Owl Tree and was surprised and pleased to see Hawk's nose back in the grain bucket. As she moved toward the tree with his hay, he jerked his head up again, but this time he didn't move away. He just watched her carefully as he chewed.

Elena felt that feeling in her gut again. That feeling she had while George and Sally were dancing in the puddle. This time it rose to her chest and stayed there for a bit, warming her heart and then warming her all over. She put Hawk's hay down under the tree and then turned to look him in the eye, still feeling the warmth.

They stood there like that, eyes fixed on each other. He with grain dribbling out the corners of his mouth as he chewed; she, shivering a little in spite of the warmth building in her chest. His ears were up and alert, pointed toward her, and she was concentrating on that warm feeling inside of her. The air felt like cool silk slipping around her and wrapping her in luxury, the evening light of dusk took on a gentle glow of gray and gold that reminded her of something that she couldn't quite put her finger on.

"I know you."

The words whispered through her mind. She looked around but there was no one there but herself and the horse. Watching him carefully, she listened for more, but nothing. There were no more words. However, she felt like she could almost see the world in the horse's eyes. As she watched him, she felt as though she were being pulled into another place and time. She seemed to be falling into the dark liquid depths of his eye. Then they were running, their hoofs thundering across a mountain meadow. Glorying in the feel of the wind in their faces, it was almost as though they were flying. She could feel every muscle rippling with movement that was seemingly without effort. Side by side she and the stallion flew across the native mountain grass.

Whoosh! A flurry of air suddenly blasted Elena from her reverie. She jumped, startled, and blinked several times trying to feel and know her human body again, trying to get grounded. Hawk was still standing his ground, looking at her, but the dream connection had been broken. As she came back into her body, shaking with the adrenaline flow, she looked around to see what had disturbed the air. There she was. The owl had come to her night place, her hunting place, the Owl Tree. The rush of air Elena had felt was from the powerful beating of Owl's wings as she had flown close overhead.

Hawk had gone back to eating. The sky had gone on with evening and darkening. Owl was ready to hunt, and Elena's heartbeat was almost back to normal even if her head was still swimming with the dream that had just taken place.

Once she got her bearings, Elena gathered up the empty grain bucket and left the corral. Lost in thought, she slipped and almost fell in the mud. *Not that anyone would notice,* she thought, smiling. Hawk had already thrown a ton of mud on her.

Dinner was a jovial occasion that evening. In honor of the monsoon, Sally had washed up the fine china that had belonged to George's mother and set the dining room table complete with tablecloth and the good silverware. She couldn't remember the last time they had used the good dishes. If they were really going to get a monsoon season this year, then a celebration was definitely in order.

Elena came in through the kitchen, took one look at the set table in the dining room, and headed up the stairs to change clothes and wash. The mud already drying on her clothes would have crumbled off all over the table cloth. She put on a clean pair of jeans and one of her new shirts. It seemed that dinner tonight was a special occasion and warranted paying a little extra attention with her grooming. She washed her hands and face, brushed her long dark hair, and for the first time since she had come to live at the ranch, she left her hair down instead of braiding it or putting it in a ponytail. Gathering up her dirty clothes to put in the laundry room, she hurried back down the stairs to see if she could help Sally get dinner ready.

12

WARM FEELINGS ON A COOL NIGHT

It wasn't long before they sat down to a dinner of ranch raised T-bone steaks, mashed sweet potatoes, and a platter of grilled zucchini planks. George was starving! Those PB&J sandwiches were long gone, and he was ready for a more substantial meal. He put his napkin in his lap, and looked expectantly at Sally.

"Wait, wait," said Sally, giggling just a little. "Has everyone thanked the rain gods for our monsoon today?"

"I'll do that after I eat," growled George in his best caveman voice. "Food! Give me food!" He reached for the platter of meat, helping himself to a large steak.

Elena looked at George, then Sally, and then George again. She didn't know what to think when they played almost like little kids, but she did know that it made her feel good inside. She had spent so much time worrying about this day. Afraid to go to town. Worried about what people would say, worried she wouldn't know what to do or say spending a whole day with Sally. And just worried about the whole future in general. What a day it had turned out to be. The knots that she had carried in her heart and in her gut had been loosened today, and she felt something that she hadn't felt in a very long time: peace. At least for now, for today. Beyond that, who knew? Tonight she would get a chance to sit with her new book. The thought excited her. There was magic in those photographs, and she was anxious to devote some time to them.

The banter at the dining table subsided as everyone fell to eating. George gave his steak all the attention he felt it deserved. When he had taken the edge off his hunger, he turned his attention to Elena.

"So. How was town? Did you find everything you needed? Where did you ladies go today besides the feed store?" He was firing off questions so fast that Elena could only sit and stare at him. "You two did a lot of shopping, judging from all the bags I carried in from the truck. Did you rob a bank to pay for everything?"

That brought a smile to Elena, but she said nothing, waiting for him to continue on. But it seemed he was done … for the moment.

Before she could think much about her answer, the words just popped out. "The bookstore. We went to the bookstore."

George looked at her expectantly, waiting for her to continue. She seemed a little bit at a loss for words after her original comment, so he prompted her more.

"Is that where you got your school supplies, then?"

"Oh, no," Elena grimaced. "We got that stuff at Walmart. We went to the bookstore for books."

"Really," said George. "What kind of books?"

"I got a new gardening book," Sally volunteered. "You should see the beautiful pictures in it."

George smiled, knowing that he would be seeing this new book after dinner, in detail. Sally's enthusiasm was one of the many things he loved about her. He looked at Elena again.

"And what about you?" He found himself very curious to know more about Elena and her interests. The fact that she was excited about a bookstore said a lot. Watching her eyes light up stirred something in him. *Those eyes,* he thought, *they are like the stallion's eyes; dark and deep until they light up with that spark of life.*

"It was hard to choose," she said. "There were so many books about such interesting things. But I wound up getting just one. It was so beautiful that it was worth putting the others I had chosen back. Can I show it to you after dinner? That would be much easier than trying to describe it."

Now George's curiosity was really piqued, and he found himself looking forward to seeing the book and hearing what she had to say about it. So he smiled and nodded and took a bite of sweet potato.

After the dinner dishes had been washed, dried, and returned to their place of honor in the antique sideboard, George, Sally, and Elena went to sit on the porch to enjoy the cool, moist night air and to look at the new books. George and Sally sat on the swing together as they did most evenings in the summer. Elena got comfortable in the wicker chair next to the swing. It was the first time she had shared an evening on the porch with George and Sally, and it felt nice. She smiled at the picture the two of them made, sitting side by side, rocking the swing gently with their feet, and holding hands. The sight made her think of her own parents, sitting together in front of the fire, having quiet conversation as she had fallen asleep on her cot in the corner.

Feelings welled up inside of her again, but she didn't feel like crying this time. The feeling started in her gut, but stopped at her heart and stayed there, warm and comfortable. She sat, savoring the feeling, as she looked into the night and listened to its sounds. Sally reached over and switched on the porch light, and all three of them blinked at the glaring intrusion.

"Well, how else are we going to see these books?" Sally asked as George and Elena looked at her, blinking in surprise. "Elena, do you have yours?"

Nodding, Elena picked the heavy book up from her lap and handed it to George.

His eyebrows lifted as he flipped through it briefly, then he turned past the introductory page to the first photograph. Immediately he felt he knew why Elena had chosen this book. The picture was a close-up shot of a horse's head, taken from the front. There was a long forelock blowing across this horse's eyes, and it had the same long, majestic looking nose. The photo suggested movement, nobility, and strength. The horse looked just like Hawk.

The photos had captions, but they seemed redundant after looking at the pictures. George flipped the pages to the next photo. It was a close-up of the horse's shoulder and front legs in motion. The way the photographer had used the light, the muscling stood out, and he could almost see rippling motion and feel the horse running.

"Well, Elena," he said. "I can certainly see why you chose this book. These photographs are excellent. Do you have a favorite?"

She nodded, and he passed the book back to her so she could find the right page. When she had found the page, she sat staring at it for a minute before she passed the book back to George. There was something very personal about this photo, and she found herself almost not wanting to share it.

George and Sally looked at the book together, and then looked at each other. Staring at them from the page of the book was an eye. A close-up of a horse's eye, so intense and alive that it almost drew them into the life of the photograph. Had there been a background instead of just white paper, they felt as though they might have been drawn completely into the world of that horse. They looked at it a moment longer, and then Elena stood up.

"It is getting late," she said. "I think I'll go to bed now."

George handed her the book, and they said their good nights.

"We will stay here a while longer, I think, and look at these books of mine," said Sally. "You go on to bed. It was a long day."

They watched Elena hurry through the door and up the stairs. Then Sally reached over and flipped the light switch off. They sat quietly for a few minutes in the comfortable darkness of the evening, both lost in thought. Then George's voice cut through the stillness.

"What do you suppose that was all about?"

"You mean Elena?" asked Sally.

"She was in an awful hurry all of a sudden. One minute we were looking at the book, and the next she was on her way to bed. I was thinking how nice it was that she had joined us after supper, because she never has. Do you think we upset her somehow?" In the moonlight Sally could see George's puzzled expression.

"I don't think we had anything to do with her mood," she said. "I think it had more to do with that book. The eye in that photo, did you notice how it resembled Hawk's eyes? Something about that eye had an almost hypnotic effect. Didn't you feel it?"

George nodded, but continued to look perplexed.

"You know," said Sally, "Elena had the option to buy several books, but she choose to buy one expensive book instead. There is something about that photograph that has captured her attention, and I think that is why she left so abruptly. She wants to be alone with that book."

64

13

SHE WAS HORSE

This always feels so good, thought Elena as she crawled between the crisp white sheets. She had showered off the sweat and dirt of the day and was prepared to snuggle into her nest of pillows with her new book. A slight breeze ruffled the curtains at the window, and she smiled as the air caressed her face. Sighing, she opened the book and flipped through the pages, looking at some of the photos she had not yet seen. But it wasn't long before she turned back to the close-up of the horse's eye. She looked closely at the detail in the photo. There were wisps of forelock hair brushing the bone just above the eyeball, apparently lifted by a breeze. Was that breeze caused by movement of the horse, she wondered, or was he standing still in the wind? She studied the picture even closer, trying to decide if the horse was in motion.

It was as though she could see every hair on his face surrounding the eye and count his eyelashes, so profound was the contrast between the light and dark of this black and white photo. But those things gave her no indication of motion. So she stared intently at the eyeball, the iris, and the pupil. There was a light, like the flame of a candle burning there. In that light, she could see reflection of something. What was it? She looked closer, concentrating on that light and reflection. She could see other horses. They were grazing on a sparse plain surrounded by tall, rock-walled mesas. Then she could smell them. Her surroundings had changed. As she looked around her hair fell in her eyes. It was when she shook her head to get the hair out of her eyes that she realized she had changed. She had hooves, four legs, a tail; she was Horse.

The herd began to move, and she instinctively knew it was time to go to water. Throwing her head up and sniffing the air, she struck out in the direction her senses told her to go. Not even realizing at first that she was leading the herd, she headed up a narrow trail between tall canyon walls made of huge slabs of reddish rock. Their hooves crunched on the gravely surface of the trail, and the only other sounds were of the warm breezes floating down through the canyon and an occasional riffling snort from the line of horses behind her. The rhythm of the hoof beats combined with the singing of the gentle winds to create a serenity that she could not remember having felt before. The trail eventually wound around the end of the tall mesa and opened up into a small, protected area within the rocks. There were a few small trees here and the smell of water was strong.

Going straight to the trees, she pushed her horse body through the branches, and on the other side was a small, spring-fed pond. Only large enough for half a dozen horses to drink from at a time, the pond fed a tiny brook that trickled down into some rocks and then disappeared.

Spirit and nature have protected this tiny oasis well, thought Elena as she stepped carefully to the edge of the pond so as not to muddy the water. When she had her fill, she moved away to let others drink. Moving softly, back through the trees, she emerged on the other side and found herself looking into the flame; the eye from the photo, now very much alive. They stood, the stallion and Elena, the mare, staring intently into each other's soul. She felt, for a moment, as though they were one; blood running through the same veins, down through their legs and hooves across the porous skin of the earth and into the pulsing brook. The stallion broke the connection to push past her, through the trees to the spring. He stopped and stood, as though waiting, then turned his head to look at her before stepping to the pond. Elena-Mare followed until she was standing next to him. The pond was perfectly still and crystal clear. The two horses stood, looking down into the watery mirror. The sun created sparkling reflections in the water and Elena felt like their reflections were speaking to them in a silent, forgotten language. She found herself trying to understand, but the images began to shimmer and then fade. The harder she tried to understand the message that she felt was there, the dimmer the reflections became, until they were swallowed up in the darkness of night.

***

On her way to bed, Sally noticed a dim light coming from Elena's room. Since it was unusual for Elena to be awake that late in the evening, Sally decided to stick her head in. The girl was propped up in her pillows, the new book across her lap, and her reading light was on. But the girl was sound asleep. Smiling, she turned out the light and left quietly. As she pulled the door closed behind her, she heard the faint *whoo hoo, whoo hoo* from outside Elena's window.

14

ANOTHER WORLD

George had found himself up before the sun. He slipped quietly out of the bed and into his jeans. Grabbing his shirt off the back of the chair where he had tossed it the night before, and a pair of clean socks, he went softly down the stairs. There was just enough pre-dawn light coming through the windows that he could see to make the coffee. He sat by the table and put on his socks and boots. While he was putting on his shirt, a loud rumbling started somewhere down low in his belly and worked its way around the perimeter and up, getting louder as it went. Shirt half on, he fumbled through the food cupboard with one hand, and worked his other through the shirtsleeve. The hand in the cupboard connected with something familiar. *Aha,* he thought. *A cookie! Perfect with coffee.* Looking briefly over his shoulder, he took a cookie, started to turn away, and then reached back in for another, and another. He stuffed the cookies in a pocket, poured a cup of coffee, and then hurried out the door, feeling like a kid and laughing at himself.

The gray stillness before the dawn was a favorite time for George. It made him feel as though he were in another world, and he could almost escape the difficulties of drought and financial hardships.

He walked over to the stallion fence to see what Hawk was doing in the early morning hours. The horse was standing quietly, his head hanging low, one hind foot cocked in the stance of a resting horse.

George had always found it interesting that horses could rest so well standing up. Nature had done that for them, he supposed, because they were flight animals. Since running was their best means of defense and protection, they did not often lie down. Only in places where they felt completely safe did they take that risk.

Hawk was not asleep, but he only turned his head the slightest bit to look at George through half-closed eyes.

Whoo hoo! Whoo hoo!

Both man and horse jumped, startled from their restfulness.

The owl launched herself from the tree and sailed gracefully away to her daytime perch. The West was beginning to glow with soft pastel hues that ran to purple as a band of gold began to color the eastern horizon. George sipped his coffee and listened to the sounds of sunrise. A couple of "hummers" went zipping past his ear on their way to the morning blooms. Way out in the pasture where the light was already beginning to warm the earth, a meadowlark song floated on the crisp air. Bluebirds and swallows came to the large stock tank in the field for their morning drinks and a breakfast of the many insects that gathered there.

As the sunlight inched its way across the pasture, he could see a small herd of antelope grazing on the hill. A coyote was trotting up the ditch alongside the dirt ranch road, probably hunting a cottontail or jackrabbit for his breakfast. Now the stallion was stirring restlessly, and George could hear snorting and nickering from the ranch horse corral. Time to feed. He swallowed the rest of his coffee and, shoving a cookie in his mouth he headed for the barn.

15

BEHIND THE WHEEL

Elena was in the between place of sleep and waking. That fuzzy place that encourages one to snuggle deeper into the comfort of the bed, even as the morning light is seeping through eyelids, coaxing one to rise. Dreams often seem more real at this time, and Elena giggled as images appeared on the inside of her eyelids. Several kokopellis, the ancient hunchback flute players that graced many indigenous petroglyphs, danced across the light, playing their flutes. Smiling, Elena opened her eyes and was surprised at the sunlight pouring through her window. She had really overslept. Realizing that she was going to be late for her morning chores, she swung her legs over the side of the bed and the book that was still on the bed fell to the floor with a loud thump.

Now Elena was really awake. She picked up the book and set it on her bed stand while memories of that eye and images of horses and sparkling water flashed through her head. She wanted to stay still and let these images gel in her mind, but she needed to get dressed, down the stairs, and out the door, so she kept moving. She pushed through the back door in a hurry and almost crashed into George as he came up the porch stairs.

"Whoa there, girl!" George grabbed her by the elbows to catch their balance. His eyes were laughing as he steadied her.

"Where's the fire?"

"Sorry I'm late. I ... I overslept this morning. I'll get the chores done right away."

George held Elena's arm and kept her from hurrying off toward the barn.

"Relax! It's OK. The horses are all fed." Seeing the worried look on her face, he smiled. "I was up early this morning, so I went ahead and fed. You aren't that late, so quit worrying. Besides, those horses aren't going anywhere. They would have been here waiting for you."

George felt her relax and released her arm.

"Did you see Sally on your way through the house?"

Before Elena had a chance to answer, the kitchen door opened and Sally poked her head out.

"I wondered where everyone was." she said. "The coffee was already made. I thought maybe breakfast would cook itself too!"

Elena, still feeling guilty for missing the chores, said, "I'll come help with breakfast."

"I'd love to have your company," said Sally, stepping down from the porch with her coffee cup. "Any special requests?"

"Pancakes!" said George. The cookies had only pumped up his sugar craving.

"How about sweet potato pancakes, then?" said Sally. She knew what he liked. "Sweet potatoes and maple flavored sausage."

Elena was already heading for the door. Her stomach was growling and her mouth watering.

Sally mixed the pancake batter and heated the cast iron skillets while Elena set the table. Elena didn't mind helping with meals. Sally was an excellent cook. She used almost all fresh food and a very active imagination in her recipes. One of Sally's dreams was to some day have a green house so she could grow more of their food right there on the ranch. Elena thought that would be a fun project. Her mother had had a small kitchen garden. But it wasn't easy to grow a variety of food in the dry desert sand.

Her mother had grown corn, squash, beans, and chile peppers. The bean plants had beautiful flowers. There had also been a small herb garden that had produced wonderful scents from both the cooking and healing herbs.

The kokopellis from earlier that morning pranced through Elena's mind again, their antics making her giggle, the sound of the flutes reminding her of the ruins on the mesa. It was as though the ancient deities were calling to her. Suddenly, she felt an intense need to go to the mesa.

Sally called out the door to George, who was loading hay on the truck for the cattle, then brought platters of pancakes, sausage, and a bowl of strawberries and put them on the table. The strawberries were straight from her own garden, and she was extra proud of them because she had been able to keep them safe from the wildlife.

After breakfast was finished, Elena cleared the table and helped Sally with the dishes. They weren't hard to wash, everyone had completely cleaned their plates and there was no food left over. As George put his hat on and headed out the door to feed the cattle, Elena offered to help him.

He thought for a few seconds and then said, "Sure, come along. You can drive the truck while I throw the feed off. That'll cut feeding time in half!"

Elena looked stunned. "Drive the truck? I've never driven before. I wouldn't know what to do."

"Time you learned then," said George. "We live we too far away from everything for you to not know how to drive, and you are legal age. Driving a truck around the pasture in low gear is the easiest, safest way I know of for you to learn."

Elena continued to look worried, and George just chuckled, tossed her cap and gloves at her, and went out the door.

At the barn, George fired up the truck and Elena opened the gate and jumped on the tailgate. They went slowly up the rutted path to the cow pasture. She jumped down and opened the gate, and then closed it after the truck. George put the truck in neutral, then got out.

"OK, your turn," he said to her. "Get in and adjust the seat so you can reach the pedals easily."

Nervously, she slid into the driver's seat and put her hand on the steering wheel. The cattle had heard the truck pull in and were starting over the hill towards them. They were walking quickly in anticipation of food and bawling at the top of their lungs. The younger calves were scampering and bucking, and the old bull lumbered along growling out his low-pitched bellow. Some of the older, tougher cows ran at the others, trying to head-butt them and push them out of the way. Behind all the rest came the ribby, old grandmas. They came slowly, staying out of the way of the mob, knowing they couldn't compete and content to just slip in around the edges when the rest were distracted by food.

"OK Elena, just slip into first gear and let it roll slowly along. I'll holler if I need you to stop. If I do, please try to brake gently and not throw me off the top of the hay stack." George smiled at her and winked.

She just nodded nervously and prayed that she didn't wreck the truck and kill George, and herself, in the process. George climbed up on the tailgate and then onto the stack of hay and hollered, "OK, let's do it!" Then he hung on, just in case.

She slipped the truck into gear and eased her foot off the brake. The truck jumped forward a little bit, but then rolled forward slowly. George pulled out his knife and cut the twine on the top bales of the stack. Then he started throwing flakes of hay out to the cattle, first to one side and then the other, as they ran alongside the truck bawling for their breakfast.

Elena kept her eyes glued to the ground in front of her, and her knuckles turned white with tension on the steering wheel. *Thank god this truck is an automatic and I don't have to shift,* she thought. She turned the truck gently when she saw the end of the fence line coming up, and about halfway back to the gate George hollered at her to stop. Not having a good feel for the brakes yet, she hit the pedal a bit too hard and the truck jolted to a stop. But George was ready for it and had braced himself. When the truck stopped, he jumped off the tailgate and walked up to the driver's door.

"OK, we're done," he said.

She started to put the truck in park and get out, but George kept his hand on the door and held it shut.

"You just stay right there and drive. It's my turn to get the gates."

"Are you sure?" she asked, thinking to herself she was lucky that she hadn't killed something already.

George smiled, nodded, winked, and then headed across the field to get the gate. Elena put the truck in drive, stomped on the brake when it jumped forward, almost bit her tongue when it slammed to a stop, and then gingerly let her foot off the brake again. This time the truck rolled forward easily, and she relaxed her grip on the wheel slightly. She rolled the truck through the gate without hitting anything and managed to stop without hitting the brake too hard this time. George closed the gate and got in the passenger side for the ride back to the barn.

Elena was still tense and silent, but by the time they reached the barn she felt like maybe she was getting a feel for it. George got out and opened the gate to the barnyard, and she drove through and stopped in the general vicinity of where the truck was usually parked. Her knees were weak and wobbly when she stepped out of the truck, but a feeling of accomplishment washed over her.

"Great job, Elena. You're going to make a good hand around here, I think." George smiled at the weak-kneed girl, trying to remember how he had felt the first time his father had let him behind the wheel. Growing up on the ranch, he had started driving at a much younger age.

A warm feeling pulsed through her like a heart beat and she flashed a slight smile of gratitude, then headed for the house on shaky legs.

Sally laughed out loud when Elena walked through the door. She could remember when her father had taught her to drive. The story of Elena's experience was written all over the girl as she wobbled through the door, and Sally was pretty sure she knew just how Elena was feeling.

"How did the feeding go?" she asked. "Take out any fence posts?"

"No, and it is a miracle," replied Elena with a crooked grin. She went to the refrigerator, pulled out the water pitcher, and poured herself a big glass full of water.

After she had taken the edge off her thirst, Elena went to the sink and washed her hands, splashed water on her face and dried off with a towel. *Geez*, she thought, and then giggled. Sally looked at her with eyebrows raised questioningly.

Seeing the look, Elena said, "The day has barely even started, and I am already sweating like I've been digging post holes all day!"

Sally laughed again.

"That is what a session of anxiety and stress will do for you," she said. "How do you feel about driving now?"

"I think I'll probably get used to it. But right now, I sure prefer my own two feet or a horse to ride." This statement set Elena to thinking about her hikes to the mesa.

Sally noticed the change on the girl's face and asked, "What are you going to do with the rest of your morning? You still have a few hours until lunchtime."

"I think I'll go for a hike up the mesa, if that's OK."

"You go ahead. Morning will definitely be the best time for that today," said Sally as she looked up at the sky empty of clouds. "It's going to be a hot afternoon. Watch out for rattlesnakes. They will be on the move looking for water."

16

BLACK OUT

Elena performed her pre-hike ritual of putting on her hiking boots and her cap, filling her water bottle, and tucking her leather gloves into the back pocket of her jeans. In ranch country, work gloves were always a good idea. Her shakiness from the driving experience was completely gone, and she headed out the driveway and through the pinon and cedar trees toward the mesa at a good strong clip. Reaching the base of the mesa, she chose her favorite deer trail up through the rocks and cactus, noticing as she climbed newly formed mini trenches where rainwater had run down the sides of the mesa.

When all of the run-off water came together in the big wash, it created a fast running river called a flash flood that ran down the narrow, dirt forest road and across one of the ranch pastures. The Forest Service would have to repair the road after a couple of these rains because it would wash out so that vehicles had a tough time negotiating it.

She watched the ground as she climbed, not wanting to step on a rattlesnake. The water had shifted things around some too, so she had to look where she was placing her feet. Stepping on a loosened rock could cause an uncomfortable fall.

Reaching the top of the mesa without incident, Elena stopped for a drink from her water bottle. She looked out across the mesa as she rested and noticed that the scenery in the distance looked distorted, like shimmery waves in the air just above the ground. *Heat waves already,* she thought. *Glad I got an early start.*

The air seemed completely still, and she could hear the buzzing of the grasshoppers that sometimes sounded like the buzzing of a rattlesnake. Until you heard the real thing. Then there was no mistaking the difference. That was a lesson Elena had learned at a very young age. There had been many snakes where she had grown up, and they would often lie in the shadows of the water tanks and rocks.

The bull snakes and rattlers looked a lot alike if you were surprised by them. But the bull snakes were good to have around for keeping the rodent population down. They did not have rattles, and they were not poisonous. Avoiding rattlesnakes, however, was always a good idea, so she had learned to be extra careful.

At least the grass isn't crunchy today, she thought as she headed out across the mesa top. There were bits of green popping up all around. The pinons had begun to grow tender green ends on their already dark green branches. The native grass was looking fresh, and even the cactus was perking up a bit. The mesa had only gotten a tiny bit of the moisture from yesterday's storm, as it was farther West. But if the monsoons kept up, the desert would come alive with flowering color.

A little spooky up here without the wind, Elena thought. *Even in this heat I have goose bumps on my arms.* Then she shivered. It felt as though a cool shadow had passed over her. She looked up to see what had cast the shadow, but there was nothing to be seen. She shivered again, and picked up her pace, excitement building as she neared the ruins.

Passing under a large old pinon tree, she nearly jumped out of her skin as the silence was broken by the scolding of a jay hidden among the branches. Now her adrenaline was running, and she was feeling really jumpy. She moved out from under the tree, and a branch snagged her arm. It felt just like fingers closing around her, and she quickly pulled herself away.

Breathe, girl, she thought. *You're letting this silence get to you.*

She walked slowly around the foundations of the old place, amazed at how much the storm from the previous day had changed the look of things. The rain had not reached this far West, but the wind had, and there were new little sand dunes that covered walls and rocks that had been visible when she had last visited, and things that had been covered were now exposed. A sense of wonder took over the anxiety she had been feeling as she gazed around the site. She began to feel a weakness in her knees that resembled the feeling from her driving lesson that morning. Still she felt wonder permeating her senses and that warmth in her gut that radiated up to her chest and her heart. Then the feeling of warmth and comfort turned to gut-wrenching anxiety. She felt the cold Shadow pass over her, and she sat down feeling as though she would pass out. Somewhere beyond the dizziness and nausea, she could faintly hear the scolding of the jay. The sound got louder as the feeling of sickness wore off, so she stood up to continue her investigation. Even as the toxic miasma was still clearing from her body, she could tell that something had changed, so she stood still and let the last of the dizziness clear. From the corner of her eye, a motion kept her still. She waited another couple of seconds to make sure her head was clear, then turned to see what had caught her attention.

She was not very surprised to find that there were people milling about, busy with their daily chores. Chores that were happening hundreds of years ago ... again. This time they didn't look peaceful, though. Men, women, and children were scurrying around, and they did not look happy. Elena felt their tension and stepped back behind a tree, forgetting that she had been a ghost in this time and place. Even after she remembered, she stayed behind the tree, watching. She felt the Shadow move again. This time it felt as if it went right through her, with icy cold fingers gripping her heart.

Now she could hear the people talking in a language that was foreign to her, but almost familiar at the same time. There was an urgency to their quietly spoken words paired with quick arm and hand gestures. Something really bad was happening here. She wanted to find out what. The cold icy fingers gripped her heart harder, and she was gasping to breathe. The jay was screaming again in the tree, the desperate figures of the people were turning ghostly, and then Elena blacked out.

17

DARK SPIRIT

Sally stepped out the kitchen door onto the porch, wiping her hands on a towel. She had been in her garden most of the morning trying to get the weeding done while the ground was still damp from yesterday's rain. Being able to just pull the weeds out of the softened ground was so much easier and faster than trying to dig them up from the hard, dry ground with a shovel.

She had just washed up from her work, was thinking about starting the noon meal, and suddenly a thought of Elena popped into her head. *Strange,* she thought. She wasn't really expecting the girl back for another half hour or so, but she stood there looking up at the mesa, watching for any movement. Nothing. Still not feeling quite right, she looked around her. Everything was quiet. Disturbingly quiet. Days without a slightest breeze were rare in that country, and unsettling. George was out working on the windmill in the summer pasture. *He sure picked a good day to do it,* she thought. Those things were miserable to work on in the wind, and it had to be fixed right away since it pumped water to the stock tank.

The ranch horses were all quietly standing in the shade of the barn, their tails lazily brushing flies out of each other's faces. Sally turned then to the stallion pen. Hawk was standing quietly, but he was alert and staring at the mesa. His nostrils fluttered slightly, and his ears were tensely pointed that way, listening for something.

Sally turned again toward the mesa, searching, looking for a sign of anything out of the ordinary. All she saw was a hawk, far away in the sky over the mesa, floating on the air currents. She looked back at Hawk, who watched the mesa for a few more moments, then snorted loudly and walked slowly to his water tank for a drink.

***

Out of her darkness, the flame appeared, far far away at first. Then it moved closer. She thought she could hear the sound of drums or a heartbeat, but as the flame moved closer she realized it was the sound of hoof beats. The flame moved closer, and was again the center of an eye. A horse's eye. Hawk's eye. He was looking at her intensely, moving toward her, encouraging her to run with him. The darkness began to fall away and she sat up, ready to get to her feet. When Elena opened her eyes, he was gone. She was cold. She was also sweating. She looked around to see where, and when, she was. There were no people to be seen, and the buildings were again nothing but tumbled, sand-shrouded foundations.

A shadow in motion almost made her jump up and run, but she looked up to see a hawk gliding in the sky overhead. Sighing in relief, she felt the cold begin to leave her body, and the dry desert heat was evaporating the sweat. She stayed where she was, watching the hawk for a few more minutes. Feeling more like her normal self, but not quite sure what normal was anymore, she stood and tested her legs. *Yup,* she thought, *they're in good working order. No jelly knees.*

She listened. *Nope, no rotten jay chattering anywhere.* The presence of the hawk gave her courage, and she was about ready to begin exploring again, but then she noticed the position of the sun. She must have been out longer than she thought, for it was directly overhead. *Whoops! Late for lunch.* Frustrated, she took a last look around, took a good long drink from her water bottle, and reluctantly headed back to the edge of the mesa and down the slope to the ranch.

What had happened in that village so long ago? she wondered. Those people had been in a hurry and working in hushed tones. From what she could remember of the scene, she was pretty sure they had been preparing for a trip.

And what on earth was that bone-chilling Shadow that had had its grip on her? Her original feeling at the village was one of warmth and comfort. But then the Shadow had taken over. It felt like it was the spirit of something very bad ... evil. She was learning that the blue jay had something to do with it. She did not know if she was having encounters with a shape shifter, or if the jay was just announcing the Shadow's presence, but he was always there screeching when that thing tried to get it's grip on her.

I am just going to have to figure out how to keep that thing away. I want to be able to find my dreams again like when I first went there. Elena was determined. *I'm not going to let that thing keep me away!* She picked up her speed then and wore off some of her frustration by running back to the house.

Sally watched Elena running across the yard and through the back door.

"Elena! Are you OK?" Sally was really worried. Elena was a half an hour late for lunch, and after that strange feeling she had earlier and now Elena running, she didn't know what to think.

"What? Yeah, I'm fine. Why?" asked Elena breathlessly.

"Well, you were late, and running...." Sally didn't mention the earlier tension that she and Hawk had encountered. She wouldn't have known what to say about it.

"Oh," said Elena, still catching her breath. "I'm really sorry. I just dozed off up there for a bit and when I woke up it was already noon."

George came in from the other room.

"Is it time to eat? I'm starving!" he roared in his best fake intimidating voice. "Last one in serves the food, but please wash up first. You look like you have been rolling around in the dirt."

Elena glanced at him a little nervously and headed for the bathroom to wash up.

"George." Sally glared at him. "You shouldn't scare the poor child."

He gave his wife an impish grin.

"She shouldn't hold up a working man's meals."

Sally rolled her eyes and put the water pitcher on the table.

"Sit down wife. The girl will serve this meal."

Since there was only a bowl of salad and a platter of sandwich fixings left to put on the table, Elena was soon seated and all were eating.

18

HAWK AND HAWK

"I think that windmill is going to need some new parts soon," said George in between building his sandwich and taking a huge bite.

Sally looked up from her plate with a worried expression.

"Oh, George, really? That is an expense we don't need right now."

"Well, I managed to rig things together for now. But I don't know how long we can hold out. Those parts are all pretty old."

"So many of the well-drilling businesses have gone under because of the drought. There aren't many choices left and the prices will be high," George said. Taking a bite of tomato, he looked thoughtful. "Going to have to shop around and see who's left to work on it. Meanwhile I'll just keep patching it for as long as I can."

Elena remained silent, feeling the heaviness descending in the room.

"Well, I think this afternoon will be a good time for a siesta," said Sally. "It is way too hot to be working outside." She looked at George sternly. "And we have tons of paperwork that needs to be done."

He rolled his eyes to the ceiling and groaned.

"Elena," he said, "maybe you would like to take business courses when you get to college. Then you can take care of all this business paper work here."

Elena looked startled. Going to college had not yet occurred to her. Not having had a real home for so long, survival issues had been foremost in her mind most of the time. Would she be here on the ranch after high school graduation? Would she even be here long enough to graduate? This was all new territory for her. But George spoke of it as though it were already decided.

George had surprised himself as well. Elena had not been here more than a few weeks, but he was already thinking of her as family. He didn't spend much time considering the possibility that she might not stay. It just didn't occur to him. He looked over at Sally who was quietly eating and wondered what her thoughts were. He was pretty sure she felt the same way he did, though.

Elena's thoughts slipped back to her morning on the mesa. What was she going to do about that Shadow? When she wanted to connect with her special place, that dark spirit, whatever it was, tried to take over. She had to come up with a way to stop it.

"Elena, are you finished eating?" Sally's voice seemed to come from far away and pierce through her wandering thoughts. "There is no point in spending the day at the table even if we are staying in."

Sally smiled and pushed her chair back. Standing and picking up an armload of dishes from the table, she headed for the kitchen sink. George wandered out to the front porch to stretch, let his lunch settle, and of course check the sky for storm clouds. There were none. He went back inside and plunked down in his favorite, overstuffed reclining chair. Already feeling drowsy from the heat and a full belly, his eyelids began to droop and it wasn't long before he was softly snoring.

Sally and Elena made short work of the lunch dishes.

"What are you going to do this afternoon, Elena?" Sally asked as she dried the last plate and put it in the cupboard.

Elena looked thoughtful for a minute.

"I guess since it is so hot, I should go check the water tanks outside. I'd hate for any of the animals to go without on a day like today. Even for an hour."

"OK," said Sally. "But please don't stay out too long. Heat stroke is not fun."

Elena put on her cap, picked up her gloves, and went out into the midday heat. It hit her like a wall as she stepped down off the porch. *Whew,* she thought. *Not even the flies will be moving much in this heat.*

There was still an element of spookiness out there from the lack of moving air, and she almost had the feeling of being watched. She looked around but didn't see anything out of the ordinary at first. There was nothing moving by the barn. The horses were all standing in what shade they could find, their only movements were swishing tails and twitching skin to keep the few active flies away. Hawk was under the Owl Tree, standing motionless. His ear was cocked toward her but his eyes were half closed and restful.

Something moved slightly in the Owl Tree. Elena looked up to see a redtail hawk sitting near the top and almost hidden in the branches. He was watching her and she smiled. Her father had told her that owls and hawks often shared hunting grounds even if they didn't usually get along. The hawks would hunt in the day, and the owls at night.

All is well, she thought. *I have Hawk and hawk to keep me company.* Smiling, she went off to check the water for the ranch horses. George had made sure the cattle had water that morning when he worked on the windmill. The horses had half a tank, which was plenty. In this heat, it was good to let them drink the tank down to almost empty every couple of days. Then she could scrub and refill it. Algae grew in the tanks when the weather was warm, so cleaning them regularly was a good idea. This tank would be ready to clean by morning.

She went back to Hawk's pen to check his water, feeling pretty sure it would still be fairly full from yesterday's rain. It was. She sat on the edge of the tank on the shady side, comfortable in the company of Hawk and hawk.

She sat thinking about her morning and the eye, and the flame and drum beats that had brought her out of the darkness. That eye had also been in her dream at the watering hole. It was also in that book.

"You are safe, little one." It was the voice. The one that seemed to come out of nowhere. "Remember," it echoed in her head, "remember."

Remember? What? she wondered.

The hawk shifted position on its tree branch and something floated down between the leaves and landed softly on one of the tree roots. Elena watched it fall without moving from her perch on the water tank. She stared at the feather.

"Remember," the voice in her head whispered. She thought she heard drum beats again, but this time it was her heart beating out the rhythm that she heard pounding in her ears.

Slowly she rose and walked to the tree. Crouching down, one knee on the ground, she picked up the feather.

"Remember." This time it was her own voice that whispered. She looked up in the tree. She remembered, then, her mother's voice.

"We are all related, Elena. Every living thing on Mother Earth. We are all One. For everything you take, it is right to give something in return and to express gratitude."

"Thank you, hawk, for honoring me." Elena wished she had something to give back to honor hawk's gift. Looking around, she saw some long pieces of Hawk's tail hair that had gotten caught on the fence. She had a plan.

The horse watched her closely as she stepped past him to the hairs and pulled them free from the fence. She noticed that he didn't move away, even though she had passed closer to him than she had ever been.

She went back to her perch at the water tank and considered the feather and the tail hairs, planning their future. For now, she carefully worked the long hairs into an intricate braid and then wove the quill of the feather into it. Then she pulled a chunk of her own hair forward so she could see, and braided the beautiful gift into her own dark, shiny strands. When she had finished, she thanked and honored hawk and Hawk.

The stallion turned his head to look at her, and briefly, just for a second, Elena was sure she had seen the flame flicker in his eye. And she felt it in her chest. A warm, safe feeling enveloped her, and she sighed. The horse's nostril riffled in a quiet snort and then he went back to his rest with eyes half-closed and his neck hanging low.

Elena began to feel a little weak and shaky, and realized the heat was getting to her. She took a good long look at Hawk and hawk, thanked them again silently, and went to the house.

The house was quiet. Elena stood inside the door, listening, and all she could hear was the ticking of the antique clock on the fireplace mantel in the living room. She took her shoes off and walked softly across the kitchen. Sneaking a quick peak into the living room made her smile. George was in his chair, mouth open slightly and softly snoring. Sally was on the sofa, a book open in her lap. She was also asleep. In the time she had been at the ranch, Elena had never seen the Laytons take time in the middle of the day to rest like this. The scene reminded Elena of the ranch horses standing together resting in the shade of the barn, and she had to stifle a giggle. Warmness permeated her middle again. Smiling, she climbed the stairs to her room to have a rest too.

19

REMEMBER

Elena sat on her bed with her pile of pillows propped around her like a nest. She had changed into jogging shorts, pulled off her socks, and closed the lace curtains partway across the window to let the breeze in and keep the heat from the sun at bay. Her new book lay unopened on the bed.

How different my life seems now, she thought. At ten years old, she thought she had lost everything. Then for seven years, she had felt nothing but loneliness, confusion, and despair. Her heart had ached with loss, and she had felt no control over her life. But now, since her arrival here at the ranch, she was finding that she hadn't lost everything. She had her memories of her parents, her brother, and her family home. Perhaps even more important, she had the teachings of her people and the reminder that she could never be alone on this Earth.

"Remember," the voice had said.

"Remember," her mother had said.

So Elena sat, remembering in her room, on that hot, painfully quiet afternoon. She remembered her home and Sam the Appaloosa and her mother gardening and baking. She remembered her father, working gently and patiently with the wild horses. And she remembered her brother, smart and handsome in his uniform, ready to go off to boot camp.

All of these memories brought happiness and sadness, but they no longer brought tears. At least not at this moment on this day. And then there was more remembering.

How she had felt walking in the desert among the sagebrush and cactus. Sitting by the gurgling stream under the huge cottonwood tree. Watching the sun rise and set as though a Master painter had taken a brush to the skyline.

I have these things here too, she realized. *All of these memories are past, present and future. I won't lose them. They are in my heart, and my spirit is in them.* And her heart warmed as she thought of the hawk's lazy circles in the sky, the trees that reached out for her on the mesa, the stallion standing under his Owl Tree, and the owl herself. They were all related, each one as important in life's scheme as the other.

Elena scrunched her brow in a scowl. *So then, where does that dark Shadow fit in? That Shadow-being with the cold icy fingers?* If the teachings were correct, and she was sure that they were, then her spirit was somehow related to that evil-feeling Shadow. And while she was not completely afraid of it, it certainly had quite a hold on her and had been very successful in keeping her from exploring the ruins. It didn't seem to want her to venture through that other world from hundreds of years ago, either.

The book remained unopened that afternoon, as Elena tried to figure out the Shadow mystery.

Stirrings from downstairs brought Elena back to the moment, and she looked at the clock. Feeding time already! Who would have thought a lazy afternoon could fly by so quickly? She changed back into her jeans and put her socks back on. Yuck. They were stiff with dried sweat. She didn't want to get out clean ones this late in the day, so she just suffered the uncomfortable feeling and went down to the kitchen for her boots.

As Elena stepped out the door, a wave of heat hit her as though she had stepped into a furnace. *Wow,* she thought. *Now would be a good time for a cool cleansing thunderstorm.* There wasn't a cloud in sight or even a hint of a breeze, but the shadows were getting long and the sun low. Surely the air would begin to cool soon. Just stepping into the shade of the barn came as a relief and she got busy with dishing out the grain for the horses.

Sally was in her garden giving it the second watering of the day. In this heat plants quickly wilted if the soil wasn't kept damp, so Sally watered before the sun was full up in the morning and after it was low to the horizon in the evening.

George was checking on the cattle and making sure the windmill was still working, but it would be hard to tell with no air moving.

Elena gave the ranch horses their evening feed, a little brushing, and some conversation. They ate slowly, still feeling the heat, but Elena knew they would finish every bit. She got the wheelbarrow out and did a little extra cleaning while they ate their grain. Then she picked up the buckets, put them back in the barn, and headed to the stallion pen with Hawk's evening meal.

The sun dropped behind the mesa as Elena went through the gate. She put Hawk's bucket down near him and then stepped back to give him space. She turned her back to the horse to gaze at the incredible light show in the West. There was layer upon layer of color just above the mesa. Stripes of gold, orange, red, and mauve streaked the horizon. Rays of bright yellow sent up from the sinking sun fanned out across the sky. Elena sighed with delight. When she turned back to the horse, he had his head in the bucket eating. He did not pull his head out and jump back as he usually did. She stood perfectly still, and he ate until the grain was gone. He pulled his head up, still chewing the last mouthful, and watched her closely. She did not move, and they stood like that, still as statues, for at least a minute before he walked back to his tree. She picked up the bucket, set it outside the pen, and came back with his hay.

Elena walked toward him, and he did not move. She set the hay down where the bucket had been and went to sit on the edge of the water tank. The horse watched her for another minute or so and then went to the hay. They were forming a comfortable routine, she thought. She hoped that soon, the comfort and trust created by this routine would allow for more familiarity between herself and this once wild creature. She longed to touch him, to groom him and smooth that dry, rough coat. She wanted to touch his soft muzzle and wrap her arms around the neck of this wonderful spirit that had come into her world.

But Elena knew better than to move too fast. She remembered

the tremendous amount of patience her father had needed when he had brought horses in from the range. And she knew how quickly all that had been accomplished to this point could be undone by pushing too fast too soon.

Dusk had brought the temperature down to something tolerable. The crickets were beginning their night song, and the swallows were darting about catching their supper of flying insects. The light over the mesa was muted now, and there was a very slight movement to the air. It might prove to be a nice evening after all. Elena took Hawk's grain bucket back to the barn. She noticed the feed truck was parked and put to bed, so she closed up the barn and headed to the house by way of the garden. The garden gate was closed, the hose rolled up and in its place, and there was no sign of Sally. Evening chores were done.

Supper was light that evening. These really hot days seemed to shrink everyone's appetite. But there was a large bowl of salad on the table with fresh greens and tomatoes from the garden, hard-boiled eggs made from fresh eggs purchased at the farmer's market, and a platter of sliced cheese and bread. And, of course, the huge pitcher of water with fresh mint leaves and lemon slices.

In spite of their siesta time that afternoon, the three of them looked tired, withered, dusty, and dry. Little conversation passed between them. It was a comfortable silence among three hard-working ranch hands. When the last plate was empty, they cleared off the table, rinsed the dishes, put them in the sink, and went to the living room.

Having had enough of the outdoors with its heat and its dust, George and Sally didn't even go to the porch for their usual time together on the swing. George fell into his reclining chair with the monthly livestock paper. Sally curled up on one end of the sofa with one of her new books. Elena went to the bookshelves on the far wall to see if there was anything interesting.

The only sound was the rhythmic breathing of the ceiling fan ... *whoosh* ... *whoosh* ... the ticking of the mantel clock, and the crickets outside. Elena took her time scanning the titles. There seemed to be a lot of old books about ranching and livestock. There was a veterinary manual, a couple of older high school yearbooks that she assumed were George and Sally's, and there was a stack of the quarterly livestock magazines. Another shelf held Sally's gardening and cookbooks, a book about building greenhouses, and another about herbs and natural remedies.

The last shelf only had a few books on it. One was a photographic book about antique cowboy and ranch gear. That would probably be fun to look at some time, but it wasn't what she was in the mood for tonight. Another was about famous ranches in New Mexico. But it was the very last book on the shelf that got her attention, *Indigenous Peoples of New Mexico*. She took the book off the shelf, sat on the floor with her back against the sofa, and flipped through the pages. There were photographs. And information about the different tribes and pueblos of New Mexico and their histories. There was a chapter about the Spaniards coming to New Mexico and how that affected the indigenous civilizations. There was also a whole section about ruins that dated back hundreds of years. Just like "her" village. Photographs of arrowheads and ancient tools and pottery filled the pages. There were pictures of ruins from incredible ancient civilizations like Chaco Canyon and Canyon de Chelly along with maps and diagrams of how the villages had been laid out. She immersed herself in the book until she found herself nodding off and trying to stifle yawns every minute or so. Finally she surrendered, stood up, and put the book back on the shelf.

Sally looked up from her book.

"Off to bed then?" she asked.

"I just can't keep my eyes open any longer. Think I'll take a quick shower and crawl in."

A growling sound drew their attention from each other to George. He was sound asleep in his chair, and the snores were breaking loose. Sally and Elena looked at each other with tired smiles.

"It looks as though we will be turning in soon, too," said Sally. "See you in the morning. Sleep well."

"Good night," Elena managed between yawns.

***

By the time Elena had showered and gotten herself ready for bed, there was a slight breeze moving the curtains at her window. She stood, looking out at the night sky and feeling the cool breeze on her face. *What a welcome change from the unrelenting heat of the day,* she thought.

The moon had not come up yet, but the stars were bright and plentiful in the summer desert sky. Elena was more interested in the air. It almost felt as though it held moisture. She scanned the star-studded sky again, looking for signs of clouds, but saw none. She decided it must just be the temperature change that she was feeling.

Sliding between the sheets gave her the same pleasure it did every night. When she had lived at home with her family, she had slept on a cot in the corner of the living room. The small adobe house had only had one bedroom, and that had been reserved for her parents. When her brother was alive, he had slept on the sofa. Elena, of course, would have returned to that cot in a heartbeat if it would bring her parents back.

Having a room of her own with a real bed, soft sheets, and a mountain of pillows was a luxury she had never dreamed of. The foster homes she had lived in always had more kids than bedrooms, so she had always had to share a room with at least one other.

She had hung her gifts from Hawk and hawk on the bedside lamp. When she reached to turn out the light, she paused for another look. How beautiful that rusty red feather was, braided into the raven black tail hairs from the stallion. She touched the tasseled end of the braid, feeling the soft silkiness of the hair. What wonderful gifts she had been given. Shutting out the light, she said a prayer of gratitude to the "hawks" and the Earth Mother.

20

THE FLAME IN THE DARKNESS

Icy fingers were closing around her heart. Squeezing, constricting. She could feel the tissue of her heart screaming for release even as it was turning to cold, hard stone. Both arms reached for the sky as she cried out. Her mouth was open, and she could feel the tension of a scream in her throat, but she could hear no sound except the pounding in her head and chest. The air turned dark, but there were no clouds in the sky.

Hopelessness! It was hopelessness and darkness taking her over. She fought and struggled against the darkness that was moving across her mind and her eyes. Then she saw the flame. It flickered in the distance, the darkness almost snuffing it out. Her mind strained to see it, and her heart beat stronger with the possibility of warmth.

It flickered again, and the darkness tried to snuff it out with those icy fingers. Her breathing switched from desperate gasps to the rhythm of concentrated effort. Her whole being willed the flame to come closer. Suddenly the flame was directly in front of her in the center of an eye. The intensity of the eye seemed to burn away the cold fingers, and as the warmth flowed through her body like lava, she woke. Her labored breath and straining heart heaving in unison. As wakefulness and reality seeped into Elena's consciousness, her heartbeat slowed along with her breathing. Her body was bathed in a cold sweat, and she shivered as she reached to turn on the light by her bed.

Crash! Startled, she almost lost her balance and grabbed the edge of the bed stand to keep from rolling off the bed onto the floor. The night sky lit up like daylight, then went dark again. She decided to leave the light off and sat up working to regain her emotional balance as well as her physical balance.

Crash! Another bright flash of light. Elena listened for the sound of raindrops on the roof, but there was no rain. An electrical storm, she thought. Her stomach knotted up. She had always hated these storms that thrived on the dry desert heat. The dark clouds formed, but they were full of electricity and released little or no moisture. The lightning from these storms was incredible and could cause a serious amount of damage.

Elena pulled the covers up to her chin and the pillows close to her ears in an effort to muffle the loud thunder. Between the adrenaline that was still running through her from her nightmare and the electric energy from the storm, she was ready to jump out of her skin.

The next crash was not so close, and the flash that followed not so bright. The storm was moving across the desert, away from the ranch.

Then Elena jumped again, startled as the door to her room opened.

Sally's calm voice asked softly, "Are you OK, Elena?"

"Yes," came the shaky reply.

Sally came in the room. "Some close hits with that one" she said, "Are you sure you are OK?"

"Yes," came the reply, a little stronger this time.

"OK then. I'll see you in the morning." Satisfied that all was well, Sally turned back down the hallway to bed. She heard George's snores before she went through the door to their bedroom.

Nothing wakes that man up, she thought, smiling. *An earthquake could open up the earth and swallow him. Still he would not wake up!* She smiled at the mental picture that brought her.

Elena sat propped up against her pillows listening to the storm move away across the plains to the East. In spite of all the shock she had encountered this night, she was surprised to find that warm feeling inside. Her anxiety gradually filtered away to be replaced by comfort. Somebody cared enough to be there for her in the middle of a storm. The thought made her feel warm and light. She remembered that not too long ago she felt she could have disappeared into the desert and no one would care. She sighed and snuggled down deeper into those wonderful pillows.

Whoo hoo, whoo, hoo. The owl's lullaby drifted on the breeze that the storm had left behind.

21

ROUND-UP

Elena woke slowly, giggling as the troop of kokopellis marched again across the inside of her eyelids. This time there was also a handful of antelope frolicking to the flute music. The whole scene resembled a clip from an animated Disney film. The entertainment marched and frolicked off into the distance, and Elena opened her eyes.

The sky outside had a pinkish cast to the gray pre-dawn light. She raised her eyebrows, swung her legs off the bed, stood, stretched, and walked to the window. Sure enough, there were clouds on the horizon.

Elena remembered her father saying if the sky was red in the morning, a storm was coming. *If that's true, I hope it brings rain instead of lightning,* she thought.

Those electrical storms scared her. They also left trees split and smoldering, power lines down, and animals lightning-struck and dead in the fields. *How powerful those clouds are,* she thought, *that they can bring greenness and life one day, and death and destruction the next.* She looked down to the stallion pen. *Good,* she thought. The tree, the horse, they were still there. She looked around more and could see no signs of damage from her window.

A breeze billowed the curtains and ruffled her hair. She sniffed the air, and this time she was sure it was rain she smelled. Last nights storm had left the air cool, and it was a relief after the previous day's dry heat.

The light drizzle started while she was doing the morning feed, and Elena was sure she felt her skin expand along with that of the earth, as though every cell was opening up to receive the life-giving moisture and begging for more.

Sally was in the garden picking strawberries for their breakfast, so Elena stopped to help. She tiptoed through the garden trying not to step on the plants.

"Well," said Sally, standing slowly from her crouched, berry-picking position. "The squirrels and rabbits left us almost enough strawberries for a decent meal. Why don't you pick some of that basil? I can put it in the eggs. And maybe a little more mint for the water pitcher."

Elena did as she was asked, and then they went to the house to get breakfast going.

The clouds were settling in, making the morning chilly, which put everyone in a good mood. George came bursting through the kitchen door.

"OK, ladies! It's time to give our cow ponies some exercise."

Sally and Elena gave him their undivided attention. This sounded like it might be fun. George looked at Sally.

"Those two old, half-wild cows with the big horns decided to go on vacation, I guess. They went through the back fence and have headed up into the forest. We need to go get 'em before they get so far up into the trees and brush that we never find them," and in the same breath he said, "Breakfast? We're going to need our energy."

Sally quickly rolled up the scrambled eggs and hashbrowns in tortillas and smothered them with green chile.

Elena set the table, thinking excitedly about the new turn of events. She had not ridden a horse since her parents had died, and she could barely contain her joy at the prospect.

They quickly ate, foregoing the normal mealtime chatter, and stacked the dishes in the sink to be washed later. The longer they waited to go after those cows, the tougher it was going to be to find them and get them home.

Sally set about getting supplies together while Elena and George went out to get the horses ready to go. She got water bottles filled, jackets and caps collected, some snacks packed, and ropes to hang on the saddles, just in case. Usually the cattle could just be pushed back home, especially with three riders to keep them moving. A rope was always a good thing to have though, in case one of the cows was injured or was extra wild.

George and Elena put halters and lead ropes on the three horse and tied them to the hitching rail. George grabbed a couple of brushes and tossed one to Elena. Grinning ear to ear, she caught the brush mid-air and began brushing Lark. Lark was a tall, dark brown horse with a soft eye and personality to match. He very much enjoyed the grooming and stood with his eyes half-closed while she worked the dirt out of his coat. No matter how much of a hurry they were in to get the cows back, it was important to get as much dirt off the horse's back as possible. A horse will sweat under the saddle pad and cinch, and the combination of the sweat and the constant movement would rub the dirt into the horse's skin and cause sores. Since the horses would be doing the majority of this work today, it sure wouldn't be right to cause them extra discomfort. Besides, Elena loved brushing the horse's coat. She enjoyed running the palms of her hands across the powerful muscles in the horse's neck, and the delicate softness of their muzzles as their warm breath tickled her fingers. She loved the way they sighed in contentment when she found their itchiest spots to brush. The horses smelled like the earth and made her think of the warmth and comfort she had found as a little girl spending time with old Sam.

George worked on his horse, Junior, and then started on Sally's favorite mount, Tweed. Tweed was a blue roan gelding. Sally swore his coat looked like a gray tweed suit. He was shorter and stouter than the other two horses. He was also very quick when it came to the stopping and turning required for working cattle. He was as solid as a tank and could hold a bull on the end of the rope if need be.

After brushing, George pulled out two hoof picks and handed one to Elena. After cleaning the horse's hooves, and checking them for any rocks or nails or other foreign objects that might lame them, George made sure that the hoof picks were tucked into the little pockets on the saddles that were made just for that purpose. There is always a possibility that a horse might pick up a stray nail or stone out on the trail.

Sally came around the corner just as they were saddling. She had an armload of supplies, and Elena hurried to help with them. After unloading her arms, Sally reached for her own saddle, swung it back, and the let its own weight carry it up where it landed lightly on the thick pad on Tweed's back. She checked the pad underneath to make sure there were no wrinkles or pinching spots, then she adjusted the pad and saddle to sit just behind the horse's shoulder blades so that his movement would not be hampered.

Elena followed suit, her father's words running through her head.

"A sore, crippled, or uncomfortable horse cannot work well, Elena. A horse that enjoys its job will give you one hundred percent try, so you want to do everything you can to ensure their comfort."

She ran her fingers between the cinch and the horse to make sure there were no folds of skin to rub and pinch. She would not tighten the cinch completely until she was ready to get on.

They loaded the saddlebags, hung the ropes and water bottles on the saddles, and untied the horses from the hitching rail. Lead ropes were wrapped loosely around the horses' necks and tied there in case they were needed later, and then the horses were bridled.

After checking the bridles and bits for fit and comfort, they led the horses out to the forest gate. George opened the gate to let Sally and Elena through, then he led Junior through and closed the gate behind him.

"Are we ready?" George asked in his best sports announcer's voice. Everyone nodded as they tightened their cinches. "Then mount up."

Looking like a choreographed dance group, they all stepped up in their stirrups at the same time, swung their legs over the back of the saddles, and settled lightly into the seats. George was very pleased to see that Elena appeared to know what she was doing thus far and was now looking forward to seeing her ride.

They set off down the dirt forest road that was more of a trail than an actual road. They were on government National Forest land now. The ranch was bordered by National Forest on two sides, which meant that the Laytons and the Forest Service shared the responsibility of keeping up their common fences and gates. That also meant that they weren't likely to have neighbors moving in any time soon except for the cattle belonging to whoever had the highest bid on the grazing lease this year and some occasional woodcutters.

Every few years the Forest Service would open up that area for people to cut firewood. That helped to keep some of the deadwood cleared out.

A short way down the road, George pulled off to the left and rode through the trees with Sally and Elena following. They entered a clearing by the pasture fence where the cows had gone through. George had quickly patched the fence earlier when he had found that the cows had gotten out, but he wanted to attempt to track the strays from here. He stepped down from his horse and handed the reins to Sally so that he could investigate the tracks. Walking a little ways to the South, he could see where the cows had entered the brush. *Smart cows,* he thought. *The ones with the horns always seem to know how to get away and how to stay as hidden as possible.* He walked back to Junior, and taking the reins from Sally, he mounted up.

"OK," he said. "It's going to be slow going until we break out of this brush."

The horses were used to the work and the country, so they headed off into the thick growth without hesitation.

Elena was glad for her heavy canvas work jacket. The clouds had settled in so low that the riders were almost in a fog, and the jacket was keeping her dry and protecting her arms from the branches that grabbed at her as they pushed through the dense overgrowth. She also wore her thick but soft leather work gloves that protected her hands yet still gave her a good feel of the reins and plenty of flexibility.

George followed the trail of broken branches that the strays had left behind them. He was wearing his Stetson, and even though the air was misty and not really raining, there was moisture dripping off the brim. The dampness in the air did not dampen anyone's spirits, however, and soon they broke free of the heavy brush.

George dismounted again to get a closer look at the tracks. He was pretty sure he knew where they would lead. There was a clearing not too far ahead, maybe a mile or so, where there was a stock tank that provided water to the cattle grazing the forest land and any wildlife in the area. Mineral and salt licks were placed near the tank, and they drew the elk as often as they did the cattle. *Sure enough, he thought. That's where they are headed.*

Mounting back up, he set off at a jog. There was no point in going too fast, as that was a good way to miss important signs. Those cows were smart, and it would be easy to ride right past them and never know it. A good comfortable jog would get them where they needed to be without wasting time or tiring the horses.

This is the best part of my job, thought George.

He sat his saddle easily, absorbing the rhythm of Junior's soft, springy jog. The motion from his horse and the moist cool air were heaven to him, and the fact that he was riding with his family to gather his cattle was icing on the cake. There was no mansion in any city that was a match for the ranch and this forest.

The hoof beats of the three horses were all they could hear as they rode. The clouds and mist around them acted like a blanket to muffle any other sound that might have been.

It's almost like another world, thought Elena. There were tiny drops of water forming on the vegetation. On the ground, there were delicate webs covering the holes where tarantulas hid waiting to catch unsuspecting prey. These webs were also catching the moisture and forming lace more beautiful than any crocheted by human hands.

Lark's dark brown coat glistened with the dampness and could have been the coat of an otter just out of the river. He had a beautiful long stride that was strong but easy to sit. Elena was beside herself with the joy of being in this moment. She watched the muscles rippling in the hindquarters of Tweed as he jogged in front of Lark across the pine-covered forest floor. Elena admired the way Sally looked as one with her horse.

Before long, George halted his horse and held up his hand in a silent signal. Sally rode up next to Junior and silently took his reins as George dismounted and carefully walked to the edge of the tree line in front of them. He stood watching for a minute and then turned to them, giving the "thumbs up" sign.

The cows were there. George walked back to where Sally and Elena waited.

"OK, ladies," he said softly. "Finding them was the easy part.

Now we have to get them home with as little fuss as possible. If they get started running, they are likely to take off in different directions through the brush, and we will be all day finding them again. We need to move slowly and easily if we can. I am going to circle wide and get behind them. One of you needs to move to the right and one to the left. As I push them forward, see if you can gently flank them without stirring 'em up. Keep as much distance as you can. If we're lucky and nothing spooks those old girls, we can have a quiet, pleasant trip home."

Sally and Elena nodded their understanding, and George took Junior's reins and mounted up.

"Elena," he said as an afterthought. "Have you done this before?"

"It has been a very long time," she answered. "But yes, I sometimes got to help my father with the livestock."

"OK, then," said George, smiling. "When we get to the ranch, we can push them into the pen near the barn. It'll be easy to take them up the lane to pasture from there."

George rode off quietly to make a wide loop and get behind the cows without spooking them. Sally and Elena split up and rode in opposite directions for a few yards where they could stay hidden in the trees until George drove the cows between them. Then the three riders could hopefully form a funnel that would encourage the cows to head toward home.

Waiting quietly in the trees on Tweed, Sally had almost lost herself in peaceful meditation when she heard the cracking and snapping of dry sticks breaking, and the staccato hoof beats of the cows coming her way. She could feel Tweed tense under her as he readied himself to do his job. Together they watched the forest in front of them. They did not have to wait long. The cows came trotting past, and Tweed angled toward them as did Lark emerging from the trees on the other side. George appeared riding easily behind, keeping plenty of distance between his horse and the cows.

The trick to riding flank, Elena remembered, was to stay far enough behind the eye of the cow so that you were driving them forward, but to move in close enough that they weren't tempted to scatter. If you got in a hurry and pushed your horse too fast, the cows would likely turn away. Success was all in the timing and having patience.

The plan proceeded like clockwork for about the first half mile. Then one of the cows decided to make a bid for freedom and broke off toward Elena and Lark. Lark wheeled on his hindquarters and lunged down into the brush before Elena could even think about it. She grabbed for his mane to keep herself in balance as the horse pulled ahead of the cow and drove her back to where she belonged. Then he snorted and pranced for a while, quite full of himself. He was good at his job, and it had been a while since he'd had the chance to show it. Elena laughed, totally exhilarated by the experience. She reached forward and patted Lark on the neck in recognition of his talent.

"Good job, Elena." said George. "You're a real hand."

Elena's heart beat faster, and she couldn't have wiped the smile off her face if she had tried.

Soon, *too soon,* thought Elena, the barn loomed ahead through the mist. The trio pushed the cattle through the gate, and Sally was the first to jump off her horse to swing it closed almost on the heels of the cows.

That was easy, she thought. *And we weren't even gone long enough to need the snacks I packed.*

"A good morning's work," George said. "We can just let these two girls cool their heels in the pen while we put the horses up and have lunch. This afternoon we can send 'em down the lane and put them back in the pasture."

They unsaddled the horses, putting the saddles back on their racks and turning the pads upside down to air and dry. Then the horses got a good brushing to get the dirt and sweat off their hides before being turned back out with a bite of grain for each as a reward for work well done.

22

COOP RUINS

The clouds began to lift at lunchtime, without having dropped much in the way of actual rain. Any moisture was to be applauded, however, and the fog and mist had left the vegetation green and water running out of the roof gutters into rain barrels. There was steam coming from the ground moisture evaporating in the noonday sun. George knew that things would soon be dry and dusty again, but for the moment he breathed in the humidity and the fresh earthy smells that came with it.

The girls had set up lunch on TV trays on the front porch.

"A shame to waste this wonderful cool weather," Sally had said. "How often is it pleasant enough to eat outside in the middle of the day?"

They were all still feeling the energy of their morning's successful teamwork, thought George. Elena was turning out to be a good hand and real help around the ranch. It felt like she was gradually becoming a part of their family and he hoped that trend would continue. Ranch life wasn't for everyone, and could be especially hard for teenagers who typically needed a social life. Elena was a rare child that seemed to prefer the animals and the land to hanging out with other kids. Of course, she really hadn't had any opportunity since arriving to meet anyone her age, so it was tough to know how she felt about it. Once school started, George was sure they would discover more about their quiet, guarded girl.

He sighed, sat back in his wicker chair, and stretched with a lazy grin on his face.

"So I thought maybe after lunch I'd start tearing down that old chicken coop."

Sally looked at him as though he had turned into a two-headed bull.

"Really?" she asked. She had been trying to get her husband on that project for two years. "What is your plan of attack? That thing is a hazard the way those old bricks are crumbling."

"I know. It was probably the fanciest chicken coop within a hundred miles, back in the day. I think it was a stroke of genius using those big hollow bricks left over from the old house. Made that a nice cool place to be for those chickens in the heat of summer. But sooner or later things outlive their prime, and those eighty-year-old bricks have had it. Think I'll dig a big hole with the skid steer, throw those ol' bricks in, and cover 'em up and let 'em go back to the earth. For now I guess we'll just have to stack the metal roofing in a pile. We can cut up the old wood beams and poles for firewood. It will probably take years to get all of the old nails and wire out of the ground. That stuff surfaces around here like every civilization for the last thousand years had 'em."

Elena had been listening quietly while she ate.

"Do you want some help with that after lunch?" she asked.

"You were already a big help this morning, Elena. I probably will spend quite a bit of time digging the hole and planning the job a little more. So why don't you just help us run those two cows up the lane to the field, and then the rest of the afternoon is yours."

She was happy with his answer. The mesa was beckoning to her, and she was anxious to try out a theory she had been thinking about.

After lunch, the three of them walked out to the barn to take the cows back up to the herd. Sally went on ahead to open the gate at the top of the lane and to keep watch so none of the cattle in the field tried to get through toward the barn. They were all at the far end of the field, but if they saw people at the gate they might think they were going to get fed and start heading in, so it was best to keep an eye on them.

George and Elena gave Sally a few minutes to get to the top of the lane. Then they opened the gate to the holding pen and shooed the two old cows out and up the lane. It didn't take much to persuade them to go. They knew the rest of the herd was up there, and with George and Elena walking behind them they broke into a trot.

Sally could see them coming her way, so she climbed over the fence and stood motionless, partially hidden by a wooden post. If the cows saw her before going through the gate, they would be likely to turn back toward the barn. They reached the gate and trotted on through, snorting and blowing and headed for the herd. Sally climbed back into the lane and closed the gate. Done! She smiled and walked toward the barn, meeting her husband and Elena half-way there.

George smiled and winked.

"Well," he said, "that job is done. Guess I'll go get the skid steer out and have a look at the 'coop ruins' project."

"He will look for any excuse to drive that piece of machinery around," Sally said to Elena. "Boys and their toys. That thing is just like a big Tonka Truck."

"Sure makes the job easier though," he said, looking fiercely at his wife. "You'd never get me to do that job if I had to dig a hole that big with a shovel."

Sally snorted and Elena chuckled.

Sally said, "I am off to do some more weeding in the garden before the ground turns hard as a rock again. What is on your agenda, Elena?"

"Thought I'd go up the mesa for a while if you don't need me here for anything until feed time."

"OK. You go on and have fun. Be careful."

Elena jogged to the house, took off her boots, and ran up the stairs to her room. She untied from the lamp the feather and horsehair gift she had received from the "hawks", then went to her dresser and removed a small item wrapped in a soft piece of cotton flannel. She put that in her pocket and then braided the feather and horsehair into her own hair. Hurrying back down the stairs, she grabbed her cap and water bottle, slipped on her boots, and was out the door.

23

THE OFFERING

Walking quickly across the driveway and crawling through the fence into the forest, Elena went directly to the trail that led up to the top of the mesa. She knew the path by heart now, but she still watched the ground as she walked. Snakes would be stretched out in the sun on a cool day, and they would be curled up in the shade of rocks if the day got warm. Either way, she didn't want to step on one.

She was also keeping an eye out for treasures that might have washed down from the mesa or been uncovered by the persistent winds. Stepping from rock to rock for solid footing in the loose hillside dirt, she zig-zagged up the hill. As she climbed, she noticed tender new greens on the ends of the pinion branches. And under trees and rocks, almost hidden, were flowering cacti in bright shades of reds and yellows. The ground had already dried from the morning's bit of moisture, and puffs of dust popped out from under her boots whenever she stepped on the dirt. Lizards darted from the rocks to hide in the shadows as she approached.

There were huge ravens in the trees that scolded and laughed at her as she passed underneath their perch. In the sky overhead, a pair of vultures floated on the air currents just passing the time of day in a gentle way.

Elena noticed all of these things, but did not hesitate in her climb. There were things to be done and she did not want to run out of time today. Especially if the Shadow thing got to her again. She was determined to get to the bottom of that problem, one way or another.

Geez, she thought as her breathing became more labored and her heart started to pound. *Good thing I'm almost to the top.* She climbed up over the edge, started to step over a small pile of rocks, and then froze. Just on the other side of the rocks was a snake sunning itself. She stood very quietly so as not to alarm it. As long as it was not coiled, it was not feeling threatened. The first thing she looked for were the rattles on the end of the tail. Yes, they were there.

She knew she should slow her body into a relaxed state so as not to alert and intimidate the snake. But her breathing and heart rate were still elevated from the climb, and she was unable to achieve the level of relaxation she wanted. Making a split second decision, she turned and walked behind the snake and away just as it coiled in alarm. She kept going, wishing to put a wide berth between herself and the startled snake before she stopped to rest.

Arriving back at the rim of the mesa, some distance from the snake rock, she found a nice pinion to use for shade. Before sitting, she walked around it, looking closely for snakes and other desert critters that might feel threatened by her presence. Finding nothing of concern, she lowered herself down against the trunk, making sure the flannel-wrapped package in her pocket was not getting crushed, and uncapped her water bottle for a drink.

From where she sat by the rim, Elena could look out over the valley and see for miles. Looking down at the ranch, she could see a dark spec moving around that was probably George with his skid-steer. The thought of him as a little boy playing with his toy trucks and dirt moving machines made her smile. She wondered what Sally had played with as a child. Then she thought about her own childhood. Her parents had made most of her playthings. She had had a family of dolls that her mother had made from cornhusks. They had been graceful and beautiful and full of personality. She had especially liked the faces her mother had painted by hand.

Her father had built her a house for the dolls. He had used cedar sticks for the frame and the vigas, and mixed mud and straw, adobe style, for the walls. Since their house had been small, her father had built her dollhouse on the edge of the garden where it was fenced to keep the animals out.

She smiled at that memory, but she also recalled that her favorite times had been helping her father with the livestock when she was old enough, and her hours with old Sam, out in the corral.

Turning her thoughts to the project ahead of her, she stood, dusted off the seat of her jeans, checked the item in her pocket again, and headed for the ruins. She walked quickly, but carefully, the snake still fresh in her mind. A light breeze ruffled the feather in her hair and caressed her face as she neared the sacred ground and her heart beat a little faster.

She paused at the crumbling foundation of what had been a large round structure, and then she slowly walked around the base of it. She had a strong sense of being drawn to this particular space, so she wanted to investigate it in more detail. Any moment she expected to hear the chattering of the jay, signaling the presence of the Shadow thing.

Right now the only sounds she could hear were the slight crunching of her footsteps and the music of the breeze blowing past her ears and through the trees. Pausing again, she looked down at the tumbled rocks that had once been walls. Then something else caught her eye.

Kneeling down to better see what was there, she reached out to brush the sand and dirt away from the object. What she had originally thought to be another small pottery sherd revealed itself to be something more. The rounded edge that she had first noticed continued down into the ground and was partially covered by a large stone. Working carefully, she continued to dig with her fingers, brushing the dirt away from the object, not wanting to touch it yet and run the risk of shattering something that had probably been buried for centuries. She worked this way for several minutes, completely absorbed in the magic of discovery, not wanting to stop until the treasure was completely uncovered.

Sucking in her breath sharply, Elena sat back on her heels and stared at her find. She was so excited that she didn't notice the cooling of the air around her. There, in front of her, at the center of her excavation, was the most beautiful little seed pot. It had some chips and cracks from the pressure of the dirt that had filled it over the years and the protective rock that sat partially covering it, but most of it was intact. The pot was white with geometric black patterns that seemed to tell a story, and she felt like it was speaking directly to her. Listening closely to see if there was a message for her from the ancestors, she suddenly heard the scolding of the jay. The chattering and screeching got louder, and her world seemed to tilt and cloud around her. Shaken and off-balance, she put her hands on the ground to help stabilize her body. Something bit into her right hand, piercing through the fog that was quickly enveloping her senses. Welcoming the pain that kept her conscious, she dug her fingers into the dirt and pulled against the biting thing. It came free easily. The object was cool to the touch and she looked down to see a most beautiful carved, flaked obsidian arrowhead, the tip of which had "bitten" her hand. A living stone shaped and sculpted by the ancestors. The sharp edges continued to bite into her as she wrapped her hand around the stone in a tight fist. The world was rocking, and the air was cold. She could feel the icy fingers trying to reach into her, but her soul fought against the attacker. With her left hand she quickly re-covered the small pot with dirt, while her right hand tightly gripped the sharp arrowhead.

The Shadow attacker was not letting up. She put the arrowhead in her shirt pocket so that she could use both of her hands to quickly unbraid the feather and horse hair from her own tangled hair. Pulling the arrowhead from her pocket, and fighting against the fog that was trying to invade her mind, she wrapped the ends of the horsehair around the obsidian blade and partially buried it under one of the foundation rocks. The braid and feather fluttered and pulled in the wind, but the arrowhead and rock held everything in place. Her breath was quick and labored and her body felt like it was being encased in concrete. The icy fingers of darkness were still attempting to get a strangle hold on her. She was feeling weaker, but she knew she had to finish what she had started.

Kneeling in front of the feather gift, she pulled the flannel-covered piece from her pocket and unwrapped it. A tear slid down her cheek as a she rubbed her thumb across the small, polished turtle shell.

Only about three inches long, it had small finger holes drilled into it and one for a mouthpiece. Her tear mingled with cold sweat as she brought the shell to her lips and blew into it. A clear, spine-tingling, perfectly pitched sound filled the air. She felt a slight loosening in the Shadow's icy grip. She fought for a lungful of air and then blew on the turtle flute again, moving her fingers on the shell to elicit a bright, fluttering scale of notes. Again she felt a loosening of the icy fingers, and this time she was able to fill her lungs more easily than before.

Her father had made this flute, called an ocarina, for her. She had learned to play at a very young age, so now her fingers flew across the holes from memory, automatically bringing beautiful, powerful song and prayer to the moment. She focused on her mind, and on the gift she had anchored to the foundation.

"Ancestors!" Elena cried in her mind and from her heart. "Listen to me. I have come here to find you and to fill my heart and spirit with your teachings. I honor you with these gifts from my Spirit allies, the Hawk and the Horse, to me, and from my heart to you. In return, I only ask that you allow me the gift of my past. The gift of family, of belonging, so that I might find and follow the Red Road into my future. I promise not to remove or desecrate what you have protected here for centuries. I want only to understand and honor your Spirit."

Elena waited, there on her knees, feeling as though her consciousness might leave her at any moment. Then she felt a slight fluttering of her heart, and the cold wind gradually became a warm breeze, thawing the icy grip on her body and soul. Her breaths came easier now. She put the ocarina to her lips and breathed out a long soul-binding note that floated across the mesa and out into oblivion.

"I play for you on this gift from Mother Earth and my father to me, and from my heart to you." Elena offered the ancestors. "This is but a small offering of my gratitude to you."

So she sat by the foundation, in front of the fluttering feather and horsehair gift, playing out her heart and soul, her pain and sorrow, her love and memories on her father's gift to her, for all the ancestors to hear. As the last note floated out across the mesa, Elena sat in silence, still feeling wrapped in a fog, but now it was like a warm, comforting blanket instead of a cold, strangulating tomb. A shadow passed over her and spoke.

Scree, scree, called hawk as he soared close overhead and then coasted up into a huge spiral on the air currant. Elena watched the hawk soar and thought about her mother's words: "Remember Elena, we are all one…. Never forget to honor those who came before you …. Gratitude and giving. If you receive a gift, you must honor the giver of the gift with something in return."

She put the ocarina to her lips once again, and trilled out a beautiful birdsong toward the sky. *Thank you for being my cousin, hawk, and thank you for the gifts you have given.* She sent these thoughts up into the heavens as she played.

24

MUSIC FROM THE MESA

Sally was kneeling in her garden, pulling weeds and pushing soil up against a few of the plants that needed a bit more protection. When she was finished with her plants, the netting and wire that she had put up to keep the wildlife out needed a little work too.

She hummed and sang as she scooped her fingers through the dirt, but could barely hear her own voice over the growl of the skid steer.

Drat that man, she thought in loving exasperation. *He should have finished digging that hole a while ago. He is having too much fun and found some other imagined chore that required the use of his mechanized shovel.* She couldn't fault him for enjoying himself. He worked damn hard every day keeping this ranch going, and he deserved to have fun. No matter what he found to do, something worthwhile always seemed to get accomplished. She sure was tired of the noise though.

Suddenly all was quiet.

Now how could he hear me thinking over all that noise? Sally chuckled, then stopped what she was doing and went completely still, directing her attention to the mesa.

What was that? I know I heard something, she said to herself. Listening intently, she heard the distant sound float down from the mesa again.

Is that the wind? I swear it sounds like a flute. She cocked her head and continued to listen. Nothing. Maybe it had just been a bird and its call had carried down on the wind. But the sound was something she had never heard before, and she had lived here a long time.

Getting up on her feet, she dusted off her hands on her jeans and went to find George. Chances were his ears would still be ringing from the engine noise of the machine, but she had to know if he had heard the sound from the mesa.

George was standing in the shade of the shed, considering the chicken "coop ruins". Now that the fun part was over, he really didn't feel like starting on the demolition project this late in the day. It always felt more like siesta time than work time this late in the afternoon. Elena's help with the feeding was always appreciated when his energy levels were more consistent with bedtime than work. He squinted and grinned as he turned to see Sally coming from the garden. The sun was directly behind her head, and he looked away, back at the chicken coop. Then she was standing next to him.

"How's your project coming? You get that hole done? I think you probably dug half-way to China." Sally looked up at him, her eyebrows raised and a crooked grin working the corners of her mouth.

"Of course," he said. "That hole was done ages ago." He looked down at her with a bland, poker face. "I decided while I had the skid steer out, I'd move those piles of coyote posts and railroad ties over to the forest fence line."

"Why?"

"Well, darlin' … cause I could." Now he was grinning from ear to ear. He slung his arm across her shoulders and pulled her close. "Looks better, don't you think?"

"Oh," she grunted and rolled her eyes. "Well," she said, "when you were done with all of that, and shut down that giant noise maker, did you happen to hear anything else?"

"What do you mean? Like what?"

"Any unusual sounds coming from the mesa, for instance."

He stared down at her trying to get a clue of what she was talking about.

"Nope. Nothing. My ears are still humming from the engine noise. What are you talking about?"

Sally sighed. "Right after you shut off the engine there was this sound. It was as though it was far far away, floating down from the mesa top on the breeze. I'm still not sure if it was real or if I imagined it, but it sounded like a flute."

"A flute? What would a flute be doing up there, and who would be playing it? Are you sure it wasn't a bird?"

"No, I'm not sure. But Elena is up there, so I am a little concerned now. What if there is someone else up there? Maybe I have been wrong all this time, and maybe she is meeting someone."

George gave her a funny look.

"Someone with a flute? She's climbing up that mesa in the heat of the afternoon to go meet a flute player?" Now he was totally confused.

"George, I don't have the slightest idea. But remember, she is a seventeen-year-old girl, and we know very little about her. Maybe it was just a bird. But it was a sound I have never heard here before."

"Well, she should be back soon," he said. "It's almost chore time. Then maybe she can shed some light on the subject."

They stood there for another minute or two, looking at the coop, and decided they were probably done with projects for the day.

"Let's go get some ice tea," said Sally. "I can't concentrate now."

***

As Elena stood up, she realized that her legs were like jelly. She stood still, trying to get strength and circulation in them again. Looking around, she noticed several jays in the surrounding pinion trees. She started to tense, but then realized that the jays were not scolding or screeching or warning. They were just flying from tree to tree and socializing with each other and paying no attention to her. What a relief. She didn't think she had the strength for another round with the Shadow thing, and she was really hoping that she would not have to deal with it ever again after making her peace with the ancestors.

Now that she was able to stand in the center of the ruins without being attacked, she spent several minutes just looking around her. She knew that it was getting late and she needed to go. But it was nice to make that decision on her own instead of having something shoving her down the hill. She studied the ground in the area of her little

116

excavation, and found the piece of flannel that she had thrown down during the struggle. She bent down to pick it up, and glanced at the loose dirt she had thrown back over the seed pot. She found another loose rock that was the size she wanted, and set it on top of the loose dirt next to the rock that partially covered the pot.

There, she thought. *Now it will not be so easy to notice where I dug. Just in case someone else comes up here.*

She wrapped the ocarina in the flannel, stuck it back in her pocket and walked back over to the fluttering feather and tail braid that she had anchored to the ground by the foundation. She offered one last little prayer, and then started back down the mesa in a ground-covering walk.

***

Sally breathed a sigh of relief when she saw Elena, all in one piece, hurrying across the driveway to the barn. She had to remind herself that she couldn't be upset with her. The girl hadn't done anything wrong as far as she knew. But Sally sure felt like striding out to the barn and giving her "what for" anyway, just to unload the stress that had been building up inside her. Besides, they needed to find out what was going on up on that mesa. She stayed in the kitchen though, working on dinner. There would be plenty of time this evening for questions ... and answers. She satisfied her frustration by banging the pots and pans around a little bit. George poked his head in the door, his brows furrowed.

"Are you OK? You sure are giving those pots hell tonight." He was secretly glad the frustration, and the pots, were not aimed at him.

"Fine," she said. "I'm fine."

George took a chance and smiled.

"You don't sound fine."

"Well, I am. I'm fine."

"You aren't going to kill the girl before you even find out if there is anything to be upset about, are you?"

She tried to keep her edge, but she couldn't do it.

"Oh, you. No, of course I'm not. I'm just so worried that there is something, or someone, up on that mesa that we should know about and don't. And I am concerned that Elena might be hiding something from us and that could be so disappointing. I want to be able to trust her."

"Did she look OK when she got home?" he asked.

"Far as I could tell. She went straight to the barn."

"And so you are basing all of this stress and worry over a noise that was probably just a bird?"

"Yes," she said. "I guess it is silly to get so upset."

But in her heart, she knew there was more to the story than a bird.

25

INTRIGUE AND THE OCARINA

Elena fed the ranch horses, giving them all a little extra grain and a bit of conversation as reward for their participation that morning. To her, there seemed to be a different energy coming from the horses since they had been out to work that day. It was a strong, confident energy that she was feeling.

Maybe it's just the feeling I brought back from the mesa with me, she thought. But she was pretty sure that wasn't the whole story. The horses had gotten the chance to show off their talents and strengths and personalities that morning, and she guessed that could be a positive experience for any living thing. Her mother had said, "Always express yourself in the best, most creative way possible, Elena! That is what Spirit and Mother Earth have done, and that is how you honor them."

She took a deep breath and let it out slowly, enjoying the lightness and strength that she was feeling. Then another presence made itself known to her. A high-pitched nicker followed by a deep grumble brought her back to the task at hand.

Poor Hawk, she thought. *He is hungry, and I have not seen him all day.*

She hurried to the barn to get his feed. As she walked to the stallion pen with grain bucket and hay, she could smell the welcoming scent of supper coming from the house, and she decided that Hawk wasn't the only one who was hungry! As if to punctuate her thought, her stomach sent up a rumble from deep within.

The stallion seemed to be glaring at her as she opened the gate to his pen.

"I know," she said, setting his bucket between them on the ground. "I haven't seen you all day. I'm sorry."

He snorted and shook his head so that his long, tangled mane flopped back and forth across his neck. She smiled, took a couple of steps back, and was surprised when he immediately walked to the bucket and grabbed a bite. He pulled his head out of the bucket and glared at her through his long, messy forelock as he chewed. She watched him for another minute and then went to the gate to get his hay. She set that down inside the pen, said good night to her disgruntled friend, and went to the house.

As soon as Elena stepped through the door into the kitchen she could feel the tension. Sally was busy fixing dinner and her back was to the door. But just the stiffness in her back and the way she was moving let Elena know that there was something wrong.

Gosh, she thought. *I wonder what happened while I was gone.* She removed her boots and went up the stairs to wash up and put on a fresh T-shirt for dinner. She carefully took the ocarina out of her pocket and put it back in the dresser drawer.

Just as she entered the kitchen again, Sally silently put a serving bowl of potatoes in Elena's hands. She turned back to the table and set it down. Sally was right behind her with a platter of chicken and as she put it on the table she announced, "Time to eat."

George got up from his chair in the living room and took his seat at the end of the table. Elena looked around the table to make sure everything was there before she sat down. Sally came back from the kitchen with a bowl of mixed veggies and took her place opposite George.

Everyone was pretty quiet as they filled their plates with food and ate the first half of the meal. Once everyone had taken the edge off their hunger, George sighed contentedly and said, "Well, Elena, I have a big hole dug out there. Tomorrow we can start tearing down the "coop ruins". You up for a day of demolition?"

"Sure," Elena said between bites of chicken. "Do you have a plan?"

"You bet I do. I'm pretty sure that hole is big enough to hold all of those bricks."

At that Sally let out a snort.

"What?" George asked, knowing full well what his wife was thinking.

"That hole is large enough to bury a village in," she said and looked at Elena. "You will have to be careful not to fall in it, you might wind up in China!"

"Anyway," George cast his wife a sideways glance as he continued. "I decided where we will stack that tin roofing. I'm pretty sure most of the wood is rotten enough to throw in the hole as well."

Silence took over again as everyone took another bite of food.

Sally stared at her plate for a few moments, trying to decide how to proceed with what she wanted to say to Elena.

"How was your afternoon hike, Elena?" she finally asked.

"It was great. I always get carried away by the view from up there," Elena answered. "Gosh, you can see forever! And now that there has been a little moisture, there are cactus flowers and tons of other things growing."

Sally couldn't hold it in any longer. She had to know.

"What else is up there, Elena?"

Elena almost answered, "What do you mean?", but she could tell that Sally was not in the mood for word games. She sat looking at Sally, and then at George. She was searching for the right words, but they were not forming easily. The mesa had been her private world since she had come to the ranch, and she didn't feel ready to share. She was going to have to, though, so she chose her words carefully.

"There is a village up there," she blurted out.

"A village?" George asked, raising his eyebrows.

"The ruins, dear," said Sally.

"Is that where you've been going, Elena?"

"Yes."

This is like pulling teeth, thought Sally. *Why is she being so secretive?*

"Interesting place, isn't it?" said George, leaning back in his chair, finished with his dinner. "They say those old ruins are about a thousand years old. Pretty amazing, I think."

Elena searched her brain for something to say. A part of her wanted to tell everything. To involve somebody else in her private world. To have a witness to the things she had been experiencing there. But the other part of her didn't trust other humans enough to share the magic. She was afraid they would berate her for being silly, or stop her from going there because of the things that had been happening.

Sally could see the girl struggling and thought, *Now what on earth is going on. What can't she tell us?*

"Elena," she said, "Is there anyone else up there?"

The girl looked almost ready to panic.

"No," Elena answered. "No one else. Why?"

George looked on in interest. It never would have occurred to him that there would be intrigue involved.

"You have been spending a lot of time up there."

"But you said it was OK." Elena was really shaken. "I wouldn't have gone otherwise. Did I do something wrong?"

Sally sighed, knowing that this was not how she had wanted to handle this, but not knowing how else to do it.

"This afternoon, while you were gone, there were sounds coming from the mesa that I have not heard before. Are you sure no one else was up there?"

Elena looked confused.

George decided it was time to get involved.

"Elena, we are concerned for your safety. Sally said she heard sounds coming from that mesa. We have no way to keep you safe if you are not here and we don't know where you are or what is happening. As far as we know you have done nothing wrong, so relax. But really, did you hear anything while you were up there? There was either extra loud birdsong coming down from the mesa on the breeze, or some one was playing a flute."

Sally was watching Elena closely and she saw a variety of expressions cross the girl's face. Stress, then confusion, and then what looked like recognition.

"May I be excused?" Elena asked. "I will be right back, I promise."

She did not wait for an answer. Quickly she shoved back her chair and nearly flew up the stairs to her room. She went straight to the dresser and pulled out the flannel wrapped ocarina.

George and Sally sat at the table staring at each other.

"I must be getting old, dear," said Sally. "What on earth is going on with that child?"

George shook his head and chuckled a bit. He was definitely curious to find out what all of the mystery was about. There was very little intrigue in life at the ranch, and he had to admit that he was enjoying this whole thing ... so far.

Elena stood in her room looking down at the ocarina, wondering what she was going to say to the Laytons. How much should she tell them? She wanted to trust them, but they wouldn't know the old stories and teachings of her people. How could they ever understand what had been happening on that mesa? She sighed and walked back down the stairs, her stomach turning flip flops.

She handed the flannel wrapped object to Sally.

"This is what you heard today," she said as she sat down at the table.

Sally unwrapped the cloth and stared at the turtle shell.

"I heard a turtle?" But even as she spoke she could see the holes that had been drilled in the shell.

George burst out laughing even though he wasn't sure exactly what was going on. The visual his mind had just received was beyond funny.

Now Elena was completely unsure how to proceed. The tension had turned to humor, and she was confused.

Holding out her hand, Elena looked at Sally. Sally put the ocarina in the girl's open hand, and Elena put it to her lips. She let out a long controlled breath, and a clear tingling note filled the room.

That's it, thought Sally. *That is the birdsong that I heard today. So beautiful. Just one single note, but it seems to fill the room with emotion.* She looked over at her husband, whose eyes were wide in surprise.

Elena felt the energy change in the room, so she let her fingers fly up and down over the holes on the shell producing bird-like trills and warbles, sometimes breathy and mysterious, sometimes clear sweet notes seeming to float through the room and out the window to fill the evening air with music. When she stopped playing, the air seemed to be holding its breath waiting for more. Elena handed the ocarina to George so he could have a closer look. Silence hung in the air for a few seconds, while Sally tried to catch up with her thoughts. Questions were jumbled about in her head and she was trying to sort them out. Elena decided to fill the silence.

"This ocarina was a gift from my father. He made it for me."

George was still turning the shell over in his hand, admiring the workmanship.

"And did he also teach you to play?" he asked.

Elena nodded.

"In the evenings after supper we would sit outside where we could watch the sunset, and my father would play. Then he would let me play. I mostly learned from watching and listening. His ocarina was larger, and it was difficult for me to cover the holes with my fingers, so one year for my birthday, he made this smaller one for me."

Sally could only imagine how special this little turtle shell flute was to Elena. It might well be the only tangible memory she had of her father. Tears began to well up in her eyes, and she turned in her chair, pretending to look out the window until the impulse to cry had passed. Finally she was able to formulate a question, so she turned back to Elena.

"What gave you the idea to play on the mesa?"

Elena thought for a minute.

"The first time I went up there, I found very old ruins. The place seemed so familiar. It reminded me of stories my mother had told me about the ancestors of our people. So I go there to remember, and it seemed like a good place to play the flute that my father made for me."

Elena had kept her answer as simple as possible. She was not prepared to tell anyone about her dreaming, or the hawk, or the Shadow, or that she played her music there in gratitude to Spirit for the dreaming and the memories.

George was enchanted. He had not been around many teenagers since he was in high school, and he did not remember ever having met one like this. Well, he thought, except maybe his wife. Who would have thought, that this girl, this orphan, labeled as a runaway, hard-shelled and incorrigible in the system, could bring such magic into their lives.

Unable to voice what he was really feeling, George said with a huge smile, "Anyone for ice cream?"

Elena, who had been holding her breath, started giggling with relief as Sally pushed her chair back to clear the dinner dishes and get the ice cream.

"OK, you two, what flavor are we having tonight?" she asked.

"Need you ask, my dear? Why chocolate, of course!"

Sally raised her eyebrows and looked at Elena who nodded yes to chocolate.

Dessert seemed like a festive occasion that night, even though there was nothing more than a scoop of chocolate ice cream and some fresh strawberries from the garden. Each of them felt like they had something to celebrate.

George was celebrating the mystery, the newness and joy that Elena had brought to the ranch. He was celebrating the fact that in spite of drought and financial troubles, he looked forward to getting out of bed every morning to see what new adventure the day might bring.

Sally was celebrating because she had learned more about Elena. She had learned something about her past and about her creativity. She had learned that she could still trust the girl, and she was celebrating the beauty of the music from that little turtle shell.

Elena was grateful that she was not in trouble, and that she had found a way to talk about her time on the mesa without having to reveal her secrets and dreams. She was celebrating the discovery that after seven long years she had found people she could talk to and trust.

26

WHAT A DAY

Elena stood in her dark bedroom looking down into the stallion pen. All was quiet from the Owl Tree at the moment, and Hawk rested peacefully beneath its branches. Clouds had moved in with the darkness, so she could barely see the outline of the horse.

Tomorrow will be our time, she thought to the horse.

Turning away from the window, she crawled into bed, snuggled down into her pillows and let thoughts of the day float through her head.

Holy cow, she thought. *What a day.* So many incredible things had happened to her! Getting to ride out that morning to find the runaways. Just getting to ride a horse again was like a dream come true. But getting to ride a horse like Lark, and herding cows too, she could not have imagined how much fun it would be. She remembered George's words.

"Good job, Elena. You are a real hand."

There was that warm feeling filling up her innards again and moving up to her heart. She smiled into the darkness. Then she thought about her afternoon on the mesa.

What a battle she had experienced with the Shadow. The memories from her mother had given her strength and wisdom to understand the mystery and defeat the cold, grasping, choking fingers. As sleep overtook her, Elena envisioned the red feather and

126

tail hair gift that she had left anchored on the mesa, seeing it flutter in the breeze, and again she smiled.

***

Opening her eyes, Elena's first thought was that it was still dark and not time to get up yet. She sighed and rolled over, wanting to go back to sleep. She grew quiet and listened, trying to figure out what had awakened her. *Tap, tap, tap,* she heard on her window and on the roof. Rain. She pulled her blanket from the foot of the bed all the way up to her chin. Her eyelids drooped, and soon she slipped back into her dreams.

***

George and Sally sat on the porch swing long after Elena had gone to bed. Neither one of them wanted to let go of the warmth and peace this day had provided. Lost in their own thoughts, they sat silently, gently rocking the swing as the crickets chirped out their evening song.

Eventually, Sally let out a long sigh as she leaned against her husband's shoulder with her eyes closed. George looked down at her and smiled.

"Interesting day," he said softly.

"I'll say. Can you believe the beautiful music Elena gets from that little turtle shell?" Sally snuggled in deeper, and George tightened his arm around her.

"This old ranch sure is a different place with her here, isn't it?" He was still hearing the flute song in his head.

"Yes her and that old horse too," said Sally. "I'm thinking it is a good thing you brought him home instead of buying that replacement heifer."

"I'm still not sure what we are going to do with that ol' boy," said George thoughtfully. "He is pretty old and a stallion, so it's not like we can turn him loose with the other horses. I'm not sure we will ever be able to handle him, and it would be a tough life for a wild horse to live in a pen that size for very long."

Sally twirled a lock of curls around her finger.

"I think that problem might well take care of itself. Elena and that horse seem to have quite a relationship going."

"Hmmmmmm ...." George seemed to drift of for a minute and then said, "I'm thinking of moving the cattle out to the summer pasture."

"Really George? Has it grown that much in the last couple of weeks?"

"It's getting there, dear. If we can get another monsoon or two in the next week that tough native grass might just surprise us. And if that happens, the winter pasture should also get an excellent start. I'd sure like to be able to stop feeding that gold-plated hay for a while. What do you think?"

The only answer he got was the chirping of crickets. George nudged his dozing wife gently.

"Come on, dear. Let's go to bed."

"MmmmHmmmm," she yawned, pulled herself up from the swing, and shuffled toward the stairs.

27

STANDING HER GROUND

Elena woke to a completely quiet house and a gold and gray dawn. The air was damp, fresh, and a bit chilly. Looking out her window, she could see patches of mist floating above the ground like miniature clouds and could hear an occasional drip of water from the gutter into the water tank below. She couldn't tell from her window how much rain had come over night, but there had been some.

She quietly got dressed and slipped down the stairs to the kitchen. She grabbed a banana after putting on her boots and vest and went outside, softly closing the door behind her.

There was a streak of gold along the Eastern horizon; the gray clouds hanging above it were slowly lifting. Soon the sun would appear and burn away the mist. But for now Elena could pretend she was somewhere besides the desert. The mist, the chill, and the gray gold of the sky gave the impression of being near a pond or a lake. She could imagine paddling a canoe or a kayak around the edges of a still pond, seeing her reflection in the glass like water. From pictures and TV shows she had seen, she could see herself pushing through the reeds and the lilies in the shallows near the shore and watching the dragonflies flit from one stem to the next.

A bright light invaded her water world as the sun peaked over the land. First to disappear was her imaginary pond, the next to go was the mist that hung over the damp ground. Water drops on the spiky native grass looked like sparkling crystals for a few brief moments before evaporating into the quickly drying air.

From the stallion pen came the sounds of Hawk crunching around, probably getting his morning drink and wondering where his breakfast was.

From the firmness of the ground Elena could tell there had not been a lot of rain, but there had certainly been enough to help the growing things take on that extra brightness and color that vegetation had a tendency to do when treated to a nice drink of water. She was sure the water tanks placed under the gutter downspouts would be well filled with water, but she would check them anyway as she fed. You never knew when a tank might spring a leak or an ambitious horse might jump at least part way into a tank to cool off and wind up throwing most of the water on the ground.

Her father had taught her that it was never OK to leave livestock without water ... ever. So she headed to the barn to get the morning's chores going.

Elena fed the ranch horses and gave them each a good grooming as they ate. She paid special attention to their backs and the girth area where the saddles might have rubbed dirt into their hide and could cause sores. She combed her fingers through their manes and tails to separate the hairs and remove any knots or tangles. Then she checked their hooves to make sure there were no foreign objects stuck in them that could lame the horses. She stroked each of them and praised them for their good work the day before and promising Lark that she was looking forward to another ride soon.

She checked the water tank and sure enough, it was full of good fresh rainwater. Picking up the feed buckets that had been licked clean, she went back to the barn to mix Hawk's feed. She put the empty ranch horse buckets on the table where she mixed their feed, so they would be ready to fill the next morning.

Hawk let out a high-pitched nicker as Elena stepped out of the barn with his breakfast. It had not taken the stallion long to learn the routine at the ranch, and he had been keeping a close eye on the barn door.

The light breeze that gently brushed Elena's face still had a hint of damp coolness left over from the past night's rain and it felt wonderful. Now clear of the early morning mist, the air was sharply clear and the colors of the vegetation intense.

Hawk, on the other hand, was a muddy mess. Again. Elena shook her head and smiled. The stallion seemed to glory in looking like an adobe brick.

His hide must be completely encased with layers of that stuff, she thought and wondered what he would look like with a good bath and grooming. She stood at his gate, looking at him and trying to imagine a clean, shiny Hawk with a flowing, well-groomed mane and tail.

Hawk was not impressed ... he was hungry. Arching his neck, he blew and snorted, his nostrils fluttering wide and spraying mist everywhere. He stomped a tattoo with his front feet, demanding to be fed immediately.

Laughing, Elena slipped through the gate with the feed bucket and set it down in the usual place. Hawk barely waited for her to back away before hurrying forward to grab a bite of his grain.

Oh ho, thought Elena. *Is he trying to establish himself as herd boss now?* As happy as she was that he was feeling easier with her presence, she knew she couldn't allow him to be bossy with her. He outweighed her by hundreds of pounds, and he was a wild thing that functioned and reacted by instinct. She needed to make sure he realized that he needed to defer to her if they were to have a workable relationship, so she only backed away from the bucket far enough to give him his space, and then she stood her ground. She too would have to learn to work from instinct, as was his way, and the herd language. But he would have to learn some of her language as well and have some respect.

Elena remembered watching her father with the wild horses in the corral. It had been like watching a dance. He had not wanted to crowd the horses to the point where they felt the need to run or fight, but he had slowly worked his way into their space, allowing them to get comfortable with his presence. It was a process of getting acquainted, learning each other's language, and establishing respect.

Hawk pulled his head out of the bucket and glared at her through his long, muddy forelock. Grain dribbled out the corners of his mouth, and he looked annoyed.

"Too bad," Elena said, standing her ground. "It's going to be tough for you, but you are going to have to give up being in charge."

As she spoke, she was filled with anxiety that he might not be able to do that. It was pure instinct for the stallion to take charge in the wild and fight for his herd. It would take a great effort on both their parts to overcome what Mother Nature had instilled in him.

In spite of her anxiety, she was also filled with elation. This was a part of the process, and they could not move forward without it. Hawk's fear was giving way to his herd personality, which meant he was recovering from some of the trauma imposed on him by the round-up and the loss of his mares. Malnutrition had further weakened him physically as well as almost taking his will to live.

Elena shivered, suddenly feeling a coldness that made her wonder if the Shadow had found her again. She and Hawk continued to look at each other. As she concentrated on his eye, she felt the cold again. This time it was accompanied by a word, a thought, a description. *Hopelessness.* She could feel that hopelessness grip her just as the Shadow's icy fingers had gripped her heart on the mesa. Another word followed. *Anguish!* Her legs felt like jelly, and she could almost feel herself disappearing. Then the feeling was gone, and Hawk had dipped his nose back into the bucket for another bite. Emotions, and words and pictures were bouncing around in her brain as though someone had turned a thousand superballs loose in a small room. She frantically tried to put them in order to stop the chaotic feeling. She closed her eyes and concentrated on her breathing, and little by little the confusion settled.

Elena opened her eyes and looked at the stallion who was again chewing and looking at her. But now, the aggression that she had felt from him earlier, was gone. She looked in his eye again and felt a wash of pain and hopelessness still, but it seemed tempered with acceptance.

"We are so much alike, horse," Elena said softly. "This place and its spirits and its people have brought me a small amount of peace. Maybe it can do the same for you."

The horse sighed quietly and continued eating. Elena went to the gate, brought in his hay, and set it down by the Owl Tree. When Hawk had finished with his grain, she picked up the empty bucket and took it back to the barn.

As she approached the barn, she could hear sounds from inside indicating that George was loading the feed truck with hay for the cows. After putting the bucket back on the feed table, Elena went to offer her help in loading the truck.

"Too late," said George. He smiled as he threw the last two bales onto the tailgate and then jumped up to heave them onto the top of the stack.

"But," he said as he climbed back to the ground. "If you want to help, after breakfast you can drive the feed truck. That sure saves me a lot of time."

"OK." Her heart was doing flip flops at the thought of driving that truck again, but there was really no way out of it, so she smiled and nodded.

"Alright then," said George, brushing hay dust from his work shirt and Levis. "Let's go get some food!"

28

EYE WITH A FLAME

Sally already had stains and dirt on the knees of her jeans and under her fingernails. She had been to the garden and picked fresh strawberries and spinach. Elena could smell eggs cooking when she came in and went to the stove to see what breakfast was going to be. She peaked under the pan lid and saw omelets slowly bubbling in the shallow pan.

"Girl, you go wash up before drooling over the food," growled Sally sternly, but with a twinkle in her eye.

Elena pulled off her boots and went to wash up, her stomach grumbling.

"Food! Where is the food!" George's caveman voice announced his entrance into the kitchen.

"You take your boots off and wash up before you touch anything in here, sir," said Sally, shaking a spatula at him.

Laughing, he scooped his hat off his head and bent over in a bow.

"Yes, ma'am."

"Who are you calling ma'am? Is your mother here somewhere?"

George snickered and went to wash up, passing Elena on her way back from doing the same.

"Watch her," he said in a stage whisper behind his hand. "She is dangerous with that spatula."

"I heard that," came Sally's voice from the kitchen.

Elena giggled. *They're at it again,* she thought. *Acting like kids.*

Sally put the finishing touches on breakfast, and they sat down to a meal of spinach omelets, cinnamon raisin toast, and fresh strawberries.

"Anyone want to take a road trip tomorrow?" asked George as he buttered his toast.

Silence greeted the question, but when George looked up, Sally and Elena were looking at him with questioning stares. Trips off the ranch were rare, and there was usually a good reason for one, so they were anxious to hear what George had in mind.

"The livestock sale is tomorrow. It will be small this time of year, but there will still be buyers there. I need to get a handle on what the market is looking like this year. The 'calf run' is not that far away, just a couple of months. I know this drought is going to affect things, I just don't know how much or in what way." He looked at Sally. "You know how much I hate shipping the calves, but it's the business we are in. I just need to get a feel for things and see what's going on out there. Do I need to sell early and get the calves off our feed bill as soon as possible? Or is the market going to go up enough for the calf run that it will be worth growing them a little longer?"

Sally thought for a minute. "Why don't we all three go and make a day of it? They have a pretty decent Cafe at the sale barn, and I could use a few groceries. We could stop at the store on the way home. It wouldn't hurt any of us to get out in the world a little bit."

"Great!" said George. "We haven't been anywhere as a family yet. It'll be fun."

Elena just stared. A family? She ate the rest of her breakfast in silence, thoughts again bouncing around in her head, making her brain a chaotic mess.

Sally was tickled at the joy her husband seemed to be finding in the smallest activities these days. She too was grateful that they had been blessed with this teen that had such spirit and grace.

But Sally also noticed the change in Elena that came with George's last statement.

Hmmm, she thought, *I wonder what is going on in that girl's head now.*

They all rose from the table to clear the dishes.

"Elena has another driving lesson this morning," announced George, looking quite pleased with himself. "Feed time cut in half."

"Lucky girl," said Sally, rolling her eyes.

Elena remained silent as she rinsed her plate and set it carefully in the sink and then went to the door to put on her boots.

Sally wondered what was bothering the girl more: their conversation at breakfast or the thought of driving again.

George handed Elena the key to the truck.

"Let's go, girl. The cattle await their breakfast!"

They walked to the barn and Elena got in the truck. She adjusted her seat and started the engine while George opened the barn doors wide. Then he walked out to open the gate to the lane, motioning to her to follow.

I have to concentrate, she thought as she took her foot off the brake and eased the truck forward. But that wasn't easy. Her thoughts kept slipping back to George's comment about family.

She let the truck coast out of the barn and through the gate without incident, stopping on the other side to wait for George to close the gate and climb onto the tailgate of the truck. Her thoughts slipped back to the breakfast conversation, and she was trying to understand what had bothered her. It had been as though someone had punched her in the gut, even though she felt like the talk of family should have made her happy.

Elena felt George sit on the tailgate, so she took her foot off the brake to go up the lane to the cow pen. The truck jumped a little, bringing her attention back to the task at hand. She concentrated on getting the truck up the lane without losing the whole stack of hay and stopped again at the gate to the cow pen.

George jumped off the tailgate to open the gate, and as he passed her window he said, "We only lost half the load of hay back there." Then he smiled and winked.

Elena grimaced and pulled the truck through the gate.

George climbed up on the stack.

"OK, take 'er slow and easy, Elena. I'll holler if I need you to stop."

The cows had already seen the feed truck and were headed their way, bawling at the top of their lungs. The calves were running and bucking, pretending to fight with each other. The bull came lumbering from the far corner of the field bellowing out in his low, growling voice.

Elena had to listen carefully for George's voice. It was hard to hear anything over the din of the herd. As the truck crawled along and George scattered hay for the cattle, Elena's thoughts turned to the discussion at breakfast.

Family. Why am I feeling this way? she thought. *Shouldn't I be happy that the Laytons consider us a family? Why does this feel so awful? I don't understand.*

A shadow crossed the windshield. She leaned forward to look up to see what had made the shadow, just in time to see the red tail of a hawk disappearing over the trees.

THUMP. The noise and the abrupt halt of the truck immediately pulled Elena's attention away from the hawk. She looked through the windshield straight at the fencepost that had stopped the truck. This was just too much on top of the confusion she had been dealing with since breakfast, and she burst into tears.

George was immediately at the truck door.

"Elena, are you all right?"

She could only sob, and the more she tried to stop, the harder and faster the tears came. All she could think of was, *I never cry! Please stop.*

And all George could think was, *She must be hurt. She sounds like she's in pain.* So he yanked the door open and grabbed Elena by the shoulders, turning her to face him. He shook her gently to get her attention and said again, "Are you OK?"

She couldn't look at him. She was so embarrassed, so she just nodded her head yes, then she shook it, No.

George was getting frustrated, not knowing how to help, not even knowing what was wrong. He reached past her and turned the ignition off, then he gently pulled her out of the truck. He didn't see any blood anywhere. Surely she couldn't be hurt, the truck had only been moving at a snail's pace.

Elena's sobs began to subside a bit.

Encouraged by this, George said, "It's OK. The truck isn't hurt any." And then was completely baffled when she burst into tears all over again. This was more than he could handle. He climbed up in the back of the truck and threw off what little hay was left. Closing the tailgate, he steered Elena to the passenger side of the truck.

"Get in, girl," he said gently. "I'm driving home."

Elena kept her head turned away from him, looking out the window. At the gates she jumped out to open them, but not a word was said on the way back to the barn.

The whole drama was a mystery to George.

Maybe Sally will know what to do, he thought. *The girl is obviously miserable.*

"Come on, Elena," he said when they had parked the truck. "Let's go to the house and get some water."

She nodded and followed, her eyes to the ground, her face still wet with tears and smeared with dirt. Her heart felt broken and she could not figure out why. It was as though the bump into the fence post had released a torrent of emotions that she could not identify or control.

Sally sat at her desk, her reading glasses perched on her nose, opening mail and paying bills. She looked up in surprise when she heard the screen door open and close in the kitchen. Taking her glasses off, she got up and went to the kitchen. George was washing up at the kitchen sink, and it sounded like Elena was doing the same down the hall in the bathroom.

"Is everything OK?" Sally reached up and picked a piece of alfalfa hay off her husband's shoulder. "It sure didn't take you long to feed this morning."

"I think we are having teenager problems," George told her quietly. "I need your help with this. She's terribly upset, and I have no idea why."

They heard Elena coming back up the hall, so Sally turned to the fridge and took out the pitcher of water.

"Let's all go sit on the porch and have a glass of water." said Sally as Elena came in the room. "I have the pitcher. Elena, why don't you get the glasses and George can get the door for us."

Once they were seated on the porch, Sally took a good look at the girl. She could definitely see the swollen eyes and what looked like pain and confusion.

"Elena, what's wrong? Did something happen to upset you?"

Elena stared at the floor, her stomach churning with the pain trapped inside her.

"No ... well ... yes." She glanced up at Sally and then back at the floor. "I ran the truck into the fence."

Sally looked at George, who nodded, but smiled a little.

"She did," he said. "But the truck was barely moving. The fence post is a little crooked now, and there's another scratch on the old truck to add to the collection of scratches and dents it has received over the years, but nothing you would ever notice."

"Well, I don't understand then. What's wrong? It doesn't seem to be anything to cry over." Sally was looking intently at Elena, who was still studying the floor, but now tears were streaming down her face again.

Oh, thought Sally. *We are there way sooner than I expected. I'll bet this doesn't have anything to do with the truck.* She glanced at George, who shrugged his shoulders with his hands out, palms up, a puzzled look still on his face.

"Elena," Sally said. "Elena, look at me, child."

Elena raised her head slightly, wearing a look of despair.

"I don't know," she said, her voice shaking.

"Don't know what?" asked Sally.

"I don't know why. I don't know why I hurt so much. I don't know why what George said upset me. I don't know why I feel so confused. And I don't know why I can't stop crying!" And the sobbing began again.

Now it was George's turn to look desperate. This girl was so special to him. He would never say anything to upset her. He didn't know what she could be referring to.

Sally glanced over at George, scowling at him.

"Elena, what did George say that upset you?"

Elena tried gulping back her tears, coughing as she swallowed the wrong way.

"At breakfast," she managed to say between gulps as she tried to stop the tears, "he said it would be our first trip to town as a family." Now she had the hiccups. *Oh great,* she thought.

George's eyes opened wide, and he looked at Sally with his mouth open as though he was going to say something, but he was speechless.

Sally sat in silence for a few moments, listening to Elena hiccup.

"So," she said to Elena. "You don't know why, but George referring to us as family definitely upset you."

Elena nodded and hiccupped.

"I don't understand. It should make me feel good if you think of me as family."

George, sitting where Elena couldn't see him, was nodding his head in agreement.

"But when I try to think of the three of us in those terms my stomach starts to knot up and I feel awful, and I don't want to." She shivered then and almost expected to hear a jay chattering a warning. Then she could see the eye. The eye with the flame in it entered from somewhere in the back of her mind and she remembered the cold, hopeless feeling she had experienced from Hawk that morning in the corral. This was very much the same feeling. Concentrating on the flame, she was able to quell the coldness a little.

She looked at Sally then, who was watching her intently.

"Elena, it's OK. You don't have to think of us as family if it doesn't feel right to you. Please do not ever think we would expect you to forget your birth family just because you are here with us."

Elena felt the knot in her stomach loosen just a tiny bit.

"George and I have never had a child of our own and it makes us happy that you are here. Does it feel OK to you if we think of you as our family? Because that is how we are feeling."

Elena tried it out in her head. Imagining herself as a guest on the ranch and the Laytons taking care of her as though she were maybe a niece or cousin or something. It seemed a little weird, but it didn't make her feel awful.

"You know Elena, once you are eighteen, you don't have to stay here with us," Sally paused, "unless you want to, and then we'll be glad to have you. So for now, maybe just think of this as an experiment."

Elena felt the knot loosen a little bit more. The eye appeared again, this time it had the rest of the horse's head with it. It was Hawk, and he had that look and feel of acceptance. She sighed and hiccupped. Looking over at George, she instantly felt bad. *He looks so sad,* she thought.

140

"I'm sorry," she said to him. "It isn't that I don't like you, and you didn't say anything bad, I just couldn't help how I felt."

George smiled at her. All he wanted was for her to be happy. He hated thinking he had contributed to her misery. He also didn't like losing the vision he had created of a happy family, so he decided to hold it close, praying that soon it would become a reality.

They sat quietly for a while, drinking their water, each lost their own thoughts.

29

MIRROR OF HER LIFE

George drained his water glass and stood up.

"Guess I'll get to work on the old 'coop ruins'. What is everyone else up to?"

Sally groaned and said, "Guess I had better get back to bookwork and bill paying. What about you, Elena?"

"I still need to clean the horse corrals." She turned to George. "Then I'd like to come help you with tearing down the coop."

"It will be great to have some company and the help," he said, "thanks."

The day was quickly warming, and most of the moisture had evaporated. That made cleaning the pens fairly quick and easy. Elena stood leaning on the rake watching the ranch horses. They were so comfortable and easy together, the three of them.

The thought came to her that she and the Laytons had been comfortable like that, each doing their own thing and yet all working together. She had been more comfortable the last couple of weeks here than she had been since her parents had died. What was it about George's reference to family that had upset her so?

She mulled over that question as she rolled the battered old wheelbarrow to the compost pit and dumped the load. Then she rolled it over to the stallion pen.

Hawk had finished his breakfast and was standing in his favorite spot under the Owl Tree where he had shade and a good view across the field. The mud that had encrusted him earlier had dried, and he had rolled and shaken the dust off. His mane and tail were still matted and tangled. He stood staring toward the horizon and barely glanced at Elena when she rolled the wheelbarrow through the gate. She scooped up the little bit of manure in his pen, thinking what a simple and easy job it was if she did it every day. Then she stood watching Hawk. He was scanning the horizon with concentration. *What is he thinking?* She could feel a tension from him and it made her feel anxious. *He is lonely,* she thought. Then something else occurred to her.

He's looking for his family. Now the anxiety felt gut wrenching. *He will never have his family again,* she thought. *Never.* Her head began to spin, her stomach cramped, and she had to clutch the rake for balance. Hawk released his fixation on the horizon to turn and look at her. Elena felt the horse's attention on her and made a valiant effort to clear the dizziness. As she struggled with her cramping stomach, she locked gazes with the horse. Gradually the dizziness and pain began to subside. As her mind cleared, she found herself standing by the hidden pool of water behind the trees. The one she had visited in the mare's body several days ago. She looked down into the pool and saw a beautiful black mare staring back at her. Hawk was there too, standing next to her and looking into the pond. Their shoulders were barely touching and she could feel his warmth next to her. The warmth felt comforting as though someone had wrapped their arms around her. Sighing, she relaxed into the familiarity and safety of his closeness. The water rippled softly in response to their soft breathing, and she wanted to stay that way, right there, forever.

The stallion snorted, startling her, and they were back in the pen, at the ranch, and she was Elena-Girl again instead of Elena-Mare.

Hawk snorted again and tossed his head. Without thinking about it, Elena took a step forward with her hand out slightly in front of her. She felt his energy pull back just a little, but his feet did not move. She stopped moving forward, but extended her hand toward the horse a little more. They stood there like that, the horse not moving, but ready to leap to safety if needed, and the girl, not moving, her hand extended to the horse in friendship. The stallion snorted and shook his head, and snorted again. Elena stayed totally still, almost holding her breath. It felt like magic then, as Hawk slowly stretched his neck, and breathing heavily through his nostrils, barely touched the inquisitive whiskers on his muzzle to the palm of her hand. Then he jerked his head up and leaped back away from her, trembling as they stood looking at each other.

Elena was elated. She so wanted closeness with this wild being whose sadness in life seemed so much like her own. She was finding a sense of family with Hawk that she was unable to accept with the humans in her life.

Why? The thought brought her up short. *Why is that? Why am I able to accept closeness from this horse, and not from the people in my life?* She thought about this while she was looking at the horse.

Another thought came to her.

I trust Hawk more than he trusts me. I am not of his herd, I am different. He has met so many others of my kind that were not worthy of his trust. Elena's eyes widened in recognition as she saw yet another mirror of her life in her relationship with this horse.

It had been the same for her since she had left her Arizona home. Everyone she had encountered had been from a different place, a different culture, and none of them understood what was in her heart. They had not understood her closeness to the Earth. They had no idea of her people's teachings and spiritual connections. Almost everyone she had come in contact with had been just as strange and different to her as humans were to Hawk. How could she trust those that had taken her from her home and had even tried to take away her thoughts, her dreams, and the language and teachings she had been born to?

She felt closer to Hawk because they were both close to the Earth. She could trust him far easier than the people she had come in contact with because his intentions were far more clear to her. Her relationship with Hawk was like dancing, with each of them taking their turn to lead and feeling each other's space and boundaries. They did not need words to communicate with each other. Body language, energy and emotion filled that role easily.

She looked at the stallion. He was still by the fence, but his snorting and alarmed breathing had subsided, and he was watching her with a softer look in his eye, his ears pointed directly at her. He was waiting. His life seemed to be mostly about the waiting.

Is he waiting only for his family, which will never come? she wondered. *Or is there something else?*

There was a good question. Is there something else? She looked back at the horse. His attention had returned to the horizon. She gazed at him for a few more seconds, then thoughtfully set the rake in the wheelbarrow, pushed it out of the pen, and closed the gate behind her.

***

George was methodically removing the crumbling bricks from the old coop and throwing them into the pit that he had dug with the skid steer. He could have just scooped up large portions of the old building with the bucket on the machine, but he wanted to sort through and remove any metal pieces such as nails and hinges. There were enough old nails of all different sizes, including huge railroad spikes, that worked their way up through the ground routinely. He jokingly referred to them as "antique" nails, and many of them probably were as they were in different stages of rusting and deterioration.

He also was enjoying the feel of this mostly mindless physical activity. There was a rhythm to it that felt good and helped him think. George had a lot to think about. When should he sell the calves? Should he turn the cattle out on the pasture or was it too soon? Would there be more rain? And what on earth was going on with Elena?

That was the biggest question on his mind at the moment. It was rare that anything took precedence over the cattle. He grinned, and then he scowled.

What is up with that girl? Sally seemed to have a little understanding of it, and they would be discussing that on the porch swing tonight.

He flung another brick at the pit and shoved some bent nails into the bucket he had brought just for that purpose. There were some large old pieces of warped plywood on the ground that had fallen when that portion of roof had collapsed. The next section of bricks would be easier to get to if he moved them so he reached down and grabbed the corner and lifted it to flip it over and out of his way. Then he dropped it just as quickly, jumping backwards and almost landing on the partial wall of bricks behind him. He was shaking and his heart was pounding as he gingerly reached down again to grab the edge. Then he caught a motion out of the corner of his eye that caused him to jump again. It was Elena coming around the corner to help him with the demolition.

Whew, he thought as he took his hat off to wipe the sweat from his forehead with his sleeve. He put his hat back on and looked at Elena.

"Getting pretty warm out here," was all he could think of to say.

She smiled, looking puzzled.

"OK," he said. "I was just getting ready to move that piece of plywood, but there's a snake under there!"

Elena couldn't help herself and she burst out laughing. George had such a squeamish, tense look on his face, but it soon turned sheepish.

"I don't even know if it's a bull snake or a rattler because I dropped that board so fast when I saw it. I do know it is a big 'un, though."

Without thinking too much about it, Elena stepped forward and lifted the corner of the plywood. Sure enough, there was a snake there, and it was a big one. But it had no rattles, and did not coil to attack, so George and Elena lifted the board all the way, and the snake took off looking for another shady cool spot some place where it wouldn't be bothered. Elena silently wished the snake safe travels as it left. After all, snakes were kin too.

George looked at his watch.

"We have another hour or so until lunch, so I guess we should just keep on."

The two of them worked side-by-side working loose the crumbling bricks and tossing them into the pit. They worked silently, comfortable with each other, and each lost in their own thoughts.

The air was warm, but not uncomfortably hot, and they could hear the clear song of a meadowlark somewhere close in the pasture. There were crows scolding each other in the small stand of Juniper trees that graced the ranch horse corral, and there was a light breeze floating across the ranch.

Elena was replaying her time with Hawk that morning.

George was replaying the scene with the feed truck and Elena, and trying to figure it all out so he could fix it. He was also thinking his gratitude that she seemed to be over her stress of earlier. It felt like no time at all had passed when they heard Sally calling them for lunch.

30

FALLING INTO NOTHINGNESS

Sally had made chicken green chile burritos for lunch. A good, filling meal that never left anyone needing more. That was exactly what was needed. The stress of earlier that morning and the physical work just before lunch had left George and Elena ravenous, and there was no conversation until their plates were empty.

Sally got up twice during the meal to refill the water pitcher, shaking her head and smiling at the appetites of the other two. She had settled for just a little chicken with chile on it and some salad. *Doing bookwork all morning is not the stuff great appetites are made of,* she thought.

They sat at the table in companionable silence for a while, letting the food and water revive their energy levels. Finally George broke the silence.

"Anyone want to go for a ride this afternoon?"

Elena sat up straight in her chair, immediately interested. Sally too was all ears. Being in the house all morning paying bills was not her idea of a fun time. She was ready for an outing ... especially on horseback.

"Absolutely," she said. "What do you have in mind, dear?"

"Since I'm considering putting the cattle back out on the summer pasture, I think we should ride out and check the fences. You know how hard the elk herds and neighbor's cattle can be on the more remote fence lines."

He sat back in his chair and thought for a minute.

"We're going to need a pair of fence pliers for each of us," he said, "some extra wire for patching, and a few bottles of water. We should be able to do this in 3 or 4 hours, but I am sure we will need the hydration this afternoon."

They cleared the table of the lunch dishes. Elena rushed through the kitchen clean-up in her excitement, grabbed her hat and gloves and was out the door, heading for the barn.

Grabbing a couple of halters, Elena went to the corral and started gathering the horses. She tied each one to a separate hitching post by the barn, making sure she didn't leave their ropes too long. If the ropes were too short, the horses might get anxious and start pulling. If the ropes were too long, the horse might get a leg over the rope and panic.

When all three were caught and tied, she went to the barn for the bucket of brushes and began grooming. She started with Junior and then moved on to Tweed and Lark.

George was carrying out the saddles, pads, and bridles while Elena worked on the horses, and Sally scrounged up the fence pliers, saddlebags, and water bottles. The three of them worked very efficiently as a team and were on their way to the pasture in no time.

The horses stepped right along, happy to be out and doing something besides standing in the corral. At the head of the bunch Junior broke into a springy jog, and the other two followed. This suited George since they had a lot of ground to cover with over a mile of fence line to check on the back fence alone.

After walking and jogging the horses for a good ten or fifteen minutes, George bumped Junior into a slow, easy, ground-covering lope with a light touch of his leg, and they soon reached their destination. Stopping Junior near the corner brace of the fence line, George turned to see if everyone was doing OK. Elena and Sally looked perfectly fine, which he had expected would be the case. It occurred to him that with the three of them, they could easily work two fence lines at the same time.

They dismounted to give the horses a break and Sally got the water bottles from the saddlebag. They sat against the fence for a few minutes, sipping water and forming a plan.

Elena felt happy and comfortable, and she wondered at this. *How can I feel so good like this most of the time, and then have felt so awful this morning over a simple comment?*

She was gazing off into seemingly nowhere when George and Sally stood up, brushing the dirt off their jeans.

"Are you coming with me?" asked Sally. "Or are you going to stay here and daydream?"

Elena was embarrassed that she hadn't heard a word they had been saying, and she jumped up looking sheepish and confused.

"I'm really sorry," she said to George and Sally. "I guess my mind wandered off somewhere."

George chuckled.

Teenagers, he thought to himself. Out loud he said, "You girls have a good time. See you in a couple of hours."

Elena took Sally's cue and mounted her horse. George headed for the eastern fence line. She and Sally were to work here on the south line it seemed.

"Let's go to the far end and work our way back," Sally said. "That way, when we are hot and tired, we are that much closer to home. We can also get a good idea of how much work is ahead of us that way."

They rode up the fence line at a jog, taking note of the places in the fence that needed tightening or bracing or replacing. There were a couple of places where the elk passed through regularly. There was telltale hair left on the barbed wire, and these sections were severely weakened and almost on the ground. The posts in these sections were loose and leaning and caused quite a bit of sag in the sections on either side. Riding on up the line, they found the top wire was broken in a few places and would just need splicing and tightening. Some of the old wooden cedar posts had rotted off at ground level over the decades, and they would need bracing with metal T-posts. George would come up with the truck loaded with posts and take care of that another time.

They reached the far corner. It was solid and the braces were in good shape, so they turned and headed back the way they had come and stopped at the first break in the fence.

Sally examined the damage.

"Elena, if you will get the wire out of the saddle bags and cut a piece about six inches long, I'll get these broken ends ready to splice."

They worked quickly and quietly for a while, getting a feel for how long the chore was going to take. After a half an hour of good work, they stopped for a water break. Fence posts made excellent back rests and they sat looking out across the field. A hot breeze blew across the land, and the grasshoppers buzzed in the afternoon stillness. Sally glimpsed movement off to the left. On the horizon, a herd of antelope appeared just topping out over the hill.

Sipping their water, they watched the antelope for a few minutes and then were back to work.

There is something so pleasing about this sort of work, thought Sally as they rode to the next break in the fence. *Out here in the quiet, working on the land. Peaceful.*

"Sally." Elena's voice broke the silence, and Sally turned to see what she wanted.

"I'm sorry for being such a pain this morning."

"You were not a pain, Elena. But I believe you were IN pain."

She is so used to hiding her feelings, thought Sally as she saw the confusion in the girl's eyes. *She has protected herself for so long that her pain feels brand new to her.*

Sally could feel the tension coming from the girl as Elena fought to subdue feelings thought to have been conquered years ago. But those feelings had only been hidden in a dark corner, and now they were fighting to come into the light. She was tempted to bluntly address the issue with Elena so that she could face her demons head on, but Sally was afraid that it might be too much, too soon.

"Elena, what's scaring you?" Sally asked cautiously.

"I ... I'm not sure. Whenever I try to think about this, everything just gets all jumbled up in my head like there are a thousand thoughts trying to get in at once. Then I start feeling sick to my stomach."

"I'm sure you miss your family," said Sally as she tightened the bottom wire of the fence.

"Yes. I miss my family and my home. It is lonely. But there is something else. More ... and then I get confused and sick."

Sally glanced at Elena. Her face had gone very pale and was covered in a thin layer of sweat.

"This fence section is finished. Let's mount up and move on to the next one," Sally said, hoping to divert Elena's thoughts slightly before the stress made her sick.

Elena was grateful for the distraction, and being horseback made her feel better ... not quite so queasy. Lark's movement underneath her seemed to capture her body until the rhythm of her heart matched his hoof beats and she could breathe easily again.

Wow, thought Elena. *It almost feels like the Shadow is back.* She listened for the scolding of jay, but heard nothing except hoof beats and grasshoppers.

"If I remember correctly, this should be our last repair on this side of the field," said Sally as she dismounted. "Good thing too, since the elk have broken all four strands of wire on this one. It's going to take longer than the rest."

To the east, she could see George in the distance, also nearing the end of his side of the fence. Looking up at the position of the sun, she guessed it was about four o'clock. She noticed that Elena had gotten some of her color back and the excessive sweating had stopped. She was relieved for the moment, but knew that this issue would soon resurface.

I hope George and I have what it takes to help Elena through this, she thought.

"OK, let's splice this wire and get headed home," she said, pulling the fence pliers out of her back pocket.

Sally saw George on Junior, loping up the fence line as she finished tightening the last strand of wire.

Good timing, she thought. *I'm pooped.*

Elena was packing away the last of their tools as George rode up.

"Well, you ladies did an excellent job. I think you had more holes to fix up here than I had on the east side." George swung down from his horse and dug his water bottle out of the saddlebag. Sally walked over, gave him a hug, and reached up to flick a bug off of his cheek. His eyes twinkled and he gave her a squeeze.

Elena smiled, watching them, and felt that warm, comfortable feeling again. Then the Eye came to her again, starting as a tiny dot way in the back of her brain and quickly zooming in to fill her thoughts. The flame was burning bright, capturing her attention, and she began to notice something in the center of the flame. As she concentrated on that center, she felt as though she were falling into nothingness, and then she found herself in a beautiful pasture with a stream running through it. She was in the middle of a herd of horses that was grazing peacefully. The water washed and gurgled over the river stones and roots of the huge trees lining the stream. Then she was back in the sun, by the fence, with George and Sally. They were both looking at her expectantly.

"Wha ... what? I'm sorry. What did you say?" Elena asked. She could feel herself blushing with embarrassment, the heat rising up her neck and into her cheeks.

George laughed.

"Are you ready to head back to the ranch? If you would rather stay and work another fence line, we could. But I think the horses would like to have supper soon."

Sally was smiling at her too. She knew the girl's thoughts had been elsewhere. Again.

"Come on, Elena, let's go."

They mounted up and headed for the trail that led to the ranch through the cedar and pinion forest. Even though most of the trees were small, the air was definitely cooler than it had been out in the field, and the forest provided relief in this hottest part of the day. The horses were hot and tired too, but they broke from a walk to a slow jog anyway, because they knew they were on their way home. They also knew it was almost time for dinner.

Elena loved Lark's soft, springy jog. It was easy and relaxing and brought a smile to her face. Sally and George were riding next to each other in places where the trail was wide enough to allow it. She and Lark were content to follow along a few yards behind, just enjoying the ride. The herd of grazing horses was still fresh in her mind, and she thought about the cleansing cheerful sound of the stream as it had rambled through the pasture. She also remembered that her brief experience there had felt a lot like the warm feeling she had sometimes when she was with George and Sally. So, she wondered. *If I could feel their love and a sense of comfort, why did the thought of family upset me so?*

She felt like the answers were right in front of her, but every time she tried to grasp them, they dissipated away to nothingness, leaving her feeling confused and bereft. Sighing, she reached down and patted Lark on the neck. *Thank you for being such a comfort to me,* she thought to him. *I very much enjoy our rides together.* Lark snorted and tossed his head. Elena looked ahead and could see the barn in the distance.

31

PLAY

After unsaddling the horses, George dragged out a long hose hooked to the outdoor water hydrant.

"The horses have worked well two days in a row and gotten hot and sweaty. Let's give them a treat and hose them off," he said, pulling up on the handle to the hydrant. "Elena, bring Lark over here. He can go first."

She led Lark closer to George, who first pointed the hose at the horse's feet, giving him a chance to feel the stream of water and get used to it before he raised the hose to rinse his neck. Then he moved it to Lark's back, adding a little extra pressure to the stream with his thumb over the end of the hose to help get the sweat out. Elena rubbed with her hand the places where the saddle had been in an extra effort to remove ground-in dirt and grit.

Sally came forward with Tweed so he could get the same treatment, while Elena found a sweat scraper to squeegee the extra water out of Lark's coat. Then she turned him loose in the corral and went to get Junior for his shower. She passed Sally and handed her the sweat scraper.

George turned the hose on Junior's front legs and slowly moved it to the horse's chest and neck. Junior kept trying to back up, and Elena wondered why he was afraid of the water. She looked at George to see what she should do. He just laughed, and she started to get indignant. He reached over and took the lead rope from her gently and said, "Watch."

He raised the hose so that the water was spraying gently in Junior's face. Instead of backing up, the horse began licking at the air with his tongue. George moved the hose and sprayed directly into Junior's mouth. They were both having a great time, George and his horse, playing in the water.

Sally came up behind her.

"Boys," she said in an exasperated voice. But she was smiling.

The smile quickly turned to surprised sputtering as George turned the hose on her and Elena, who squealed and ducked. Sally ran under Junior's neck and grabbed at the hose. She wasn't quite quick enough though, and got sprayed again.

Junior decided he had had enough of this horseplay and flung his head back, pulling the rope from George's hands. Then he trotted a few feet away, out of the war zone, and dropped his head to graze. While George was grabbing Sally, Elena, under a rain of spray from the hose, went to catch Junior. She passed the hydrant as she went and had the presence of mind to shove the handle down and shut off the water.

George scowled in play, and directed his attention to his struggling wife. He had a hold of her around her waist. As she pulled to get loose, he abruptly let go and she almost went face first into the mud.

"You will pay for this George Layton," Sally growled playfully. "You had better watch your back, buster."

George waved an arm at her as though to dismiss her threats, then turned to walk past her to the barn, smiling smugly. Until he went face first into the mud. Sally had stuck her foot out as he walked by and tripped him. Now it was her turn to be smug.

"What'd I tell you," she said, looking down at him with her hands on her hips.

Suddenly her feet were swept right out from under her, and she went down, half of her landed in the mud, and the other half on top of her husband, who was sneering at her.

Elena took Junior to the corral and turned him loose. When she came back around the corner of the barn, there were the two adults, lying in the mud, trying to rub each other's face in it. She grabbed the hose, pulled up the handle on the hydrant, and sprayed the two mud wrestlers. They both turned to look at her in surprise, and she was afraid maybe she had gone too far. But George jumped up, pulling his wife with him.

"Great idea, girl! Come on then, hose this mud off of us."

Elena hosed the mud off of them, giggling the whole time.

They look like Hawk, she thought, *when he rolls in the mud after a rain.* Adobe bricks.

Finally everyone was soaked, but clean of the mud, so they went ahead and started chores. The sun was still hot enough to dry them before they were finished.

32

THE FLAME IN HIS EYES

Elena decided not to spend too much time with any of the horses at feeding time. She needed to get cleaned up before dinner, so she decided she would pay a visit to Hawk later in the evening. She took his feed and put the grain bucket down in the usual spot. Backing up a couple of steps, she waited for him to eat his grain. He stood, unmoving, under the tree for a minute or two, just looking at her.

"Are you going to eat?" she asked him. "I have to go eat my dinner too, you know."

The stallion snorted, shook his head, and stepped forward to the bucket. Once there, he didn't waste any time diving into his grain, and he ate like she wasn't even there. When he finished, she went to get his hay from outside the gate, and he went back to his spot under the tree. She set the hay down and picked up the bucket.

"You have a good dinner. I'll be back after I have mine."

Elena took the bucket to the barn and hurried to the house to get cleaned up. As she passed through the kitchen, Sally called to her.

"I'll be doing laundry tonight, Elena. So after you change, just throw your dirty clothes in the laundry room."

"OK," she replied as she headed up the stairs.

She stripped down and jumped in the shower for a couple of minutes. Putting on a fresh T-shirt and jeans, she slipped on a clean pair of socks and went to help with dinner.

"If you want to, watch the rice so it doesn't boil over and make sure that the chicken doesn't burn, I'll run and get cleaned up," Sally said to Elena, handing her the fork she was using to turn the chicken.

Just as Sally turned to the stairway, George came through the kitchen door, and he was covered in dried mud and loose hay dust.

"George, you go straight to the laundry room and strip. I will bring you something clean to change into there. And be careful that you don't let that dirt crumble all over my kitchen floor on your way."

George rolled his eyes and made brushing motions with his hands, pretending to brush the dirt off where he stood.

"Boys," said Sally as she went up the stairs.

Elena smiled as she poked the fork at the chicken sizzling in the pan.

George tip-toed to the laundry room and closed the door behind him.

They were all extra hungry by the time they sat down to a dinner of chicken and rice with a Frangelico cream sauce and sliced cucumbers, carrots, and bell peppers. They ate quietly for a few minutes.

"Well," said George, his plate half empty, "what time should we leave tomorrow? The sale starts at 11:00, takes about an hour to get there." He stabbed a few slices of cucumber.

"So we should be able to just do our chores, clean up and go," Sally said thoughtfully. "It should be an easy day. Do we need anything besides a few groceries?"

They all sat thinking for a bit, and then shook their heads.

"Good. We can have lunch at the sale barn. They make really good chile there."

"Chile burgers," said George, rubbing his stomach as though he was starving even though he had just cleaned his plate. "Chile burgers and a big pile of fries."

He had such a look of happiness and contentment at the thought of chile burgers that both Sally and Elena busted out laughing.

"You would think that the man never eats," said Sally.

"Good chile burgers are few and far between, my dear. Don't deny a working man his simple pleasures."

Sally looked up at the ceiling briefly, and then popped the last of her bell pepper slices in her mouth.

There was still light in the sky after the dinner clean up was finished. The sun was getting pretty low on the horizon, and the sky was beginning to streak with color.

Good, thought Elena. *I should have just enough light to spend some time with Hawk.* Not that she really needed much light, but she was so interested in reading his eyes, and that would be tough in the dark.

Sally wiped her hands on the towel that hung on the handle of the stove.

"We are headed for our porch swing, Elena. Care to join us?"

"I would like that, but I didn't get to spend any time with Hawk this afternoon. Would you mind if I go see him instead?"

"Of course we don't mind. You go right ahead. Watch for snakes though. You know they get out and about at night while the air is cool." Sally gave her a tired grin and went through the living room to the porch.

Elena slipped on her barn shoes and went to see her friend.

Whoo hoo, whoo hoo. The owl greeted her as she climbed over the fence into Hawk's corral. She smiled up at her feathered, nocturnal friend.

"Greetings to you too, cousin."

As she passed Hawk's water tank, she took note that it was ready for scrubbing. *Have to do that quickly in the morning before we leave,* she thought. Filling it would take some time.

The sun was low enough on the horizon to turn everything shades of gray and purple, even the air seemed to move in muted mauve shadows. There was just that small strip of golden light on the western horizon. The final wave from the sun before setting behind the mesa and heading for other parts of the world.

As the sun set, a nearly full moon was rising in the East, creating a different light backdrop for the shadows. The effect was breathtaking, and Elena just stood for a while in the middle of the corral enjoying the evening.

Hawk stood under the Owl Tree watching the eastern horizon. As the sun dropped below the mesa and the moon rose higher, his silhouetted figure took on a ghostly appearance. Then he turned to look at Elena, and in spite of the darkness and shadows, the flicker of that flame could be seen clearly in his eye. It seemed to her that the moon and the sun were reflected there, exclusively in that one small point.

She was completely absorbed by that phenomenon, and soon felt herself falling into the fiery heat of the flame.

The air was hot and stifling. Sun was reflecting from what looked like an endless desert. She was running at a pace she felt as though she could not maintain for long. As her breathing became more labored, she heard the sound of muffled hoof beats around her, and the breathing of many as they ran as a herd across the heated sand. She could see the stallion up ahead, trying to lead his herd to safety. She did not yet know the source of the danger and did not dare to slow down to look back. Her black mane and tail billowed out behind her as she ran, and she could feel the sweat pop out all over her black hide before it disappeared, evaporated in the dry heat.

The herd labored up the next dune that rose from the desert floor. In front of them were boxes built of wooden rails. The herd tried to scatter. The stallion veered off to the right, trying to lead them around the trap, but there was another box there.

As the herd milled around, Elena-Mare could see the threat they had been running from. There were men on horseback. They wore flowing robes that billowed out behind them as they ran their horses at the herd, cracking whips and yelling.

In fear and frenzy, the herd, having nowhere else to go, fled into the traps and gates were thrown closed. The herd milled around in the tight quarters. Necks stretched and heads thrown up, they rolled their eyes trying to find a leader, desperately trying to find a way out.

As the herd began to quiet from exhaustion, she heard a commotion from the other pen. There was shouting and more chaos, and then she could hear the stallion scream above the human noises. She pushed her way through the herd, stumbling in her exhaustion and thirst, trying to find the stallion. Reaching the fence on the other side, she almost wished she hadn't.

The stallion reared high above the men, fighting desperately against the ropes that encircled his neck. There were many ropes held by the men, and they were tightening around his windpipe and choking him down. She watched in horror as he fell sideways into the hot sand, gasping for air as the light began to disappear from his eyes.

Her heart felt as though it would burst from the pain, and she felt herself falling too. But as she landed, she felt firm earth beneath her. She stayed still, trying to catch her breath. As she concentrated on her breathing, she felt cool air settling around her and, opening her eyes, realized that she was back in the stallion pen on the ranch. Still standing right where she had been watching the moon rise in Hawk's eyes.

She needed to steady herself as her legs felt like jelly underneath her. She moved to the water tank and lowered herself until she was resting against it, but she never took her eyes off the stallions. The flame was still there, glowing and flickering brightly. He stared at her intently, and she heard the voice again.

"More. There is more."

And then, barely having had time to catch her breath, she felt herself falling again.

And again she was running. Again she could hear the sound of hoof beats all around her, but this time it sounded like thunder as they ran frantically over rocks and hard-packed ground. Their hides were scratched and ripped open as they ran through trees and thick brush. Her black coat was covered in white lather as they burst from the trees into open land covered in cactus and sagebrush.

They ran as far as they could, until they were stopped by a towering rock wall that turned the herd and led to a box canyon. The stallion tried to turn and find a way out. But there was no way out. The herd milled around and around in confused panic. Then there was a loud roar and a flash of light. Then another, and another, and she watched her herd mates, her family, dropping to the ground all around her. And then she was falling, and falling, and it felt like she would never stop.

She did stop. She could feel water. Her hands seemed frozen in spite of the sweat she could feel pouring down her face. Opening her eyes, the first thing she saw was Hawk, and then she felt a wave of relief wash through her like a cleansing rain. She was still half-leaning, half-sitting against the water tank. Her hands had a death grip on the edges of the tank and were partially in the water.

Elena closed her eyes, trying to bring herself into this reality again. Then she opened them, and looking into Hawk's eye she realized that it wasn't to be.

No! she thought. *No more! I'm too exhausted. I don't think I can take any more.* Then there was blackness.

She was falling. She was running, surrounded by the herd. It was like instant replay that she couldn't control. Again they were thundering through the trees, over rocks, hides being torn and ripped by grasping tree branches and thick underbrush. Again, they burst from the tree cover into a huge open plain covered in sage and cactus.

A loud, unwavering, unforgiving roar filled Elena-Mare's head as a huge shadow covered the herd and seemed to fill the universe. *Terror! Panic!* She felt as though she couldn't run another step, but they couldn't stop. The roaring shadow would envelope them with darkness, and it would all be over.

Running in terror, trying to escape the roaring shadow, she again looked for the stallion. He was running in his place at the front of the panicked herd, trying desperately to lead them to safety. Ahead she could see a rock wall. They were again being run into a box canyon. This time there were also cedar rails, cut from the nearby forest.

Elena waited for the roar and the shooting flames from before, but they didn't come. Instead, a man on horseback galloped up and slammed the gate hanging from the cedar poles shut. The roaring shadow moved away and faded into oblivion, leaving behind a large pen filled with confused, panicked, exhausted horses.

Elena-Mare fought to catch her breath and was then filled with overwhelming emotion and pain. Her head was filled with the chaos and cries of the herd as they tried to find their mothers, friends, and babies. She heard the stallion scream over the din and opened her eyes long enough to see him rearing above the herd, his neck again encircled by choking ropes. Closing her eyes again, she prayed for it to end.

She was crying, sobbing, her heart breaking into a million pieces, tears streaming from her eyes as she opened them to see Hawk, standing in front of her, not having moved at all. The only change was that the fiery flame in his eye had dimmed, and he wore a look of exhaustion that appeared to match her own.

The next thing she felt was a sense of gratitude and comfort. A picture drifted quietly through her mind of two horses grazing in a peaceful meadow with a stream flowing through it, bubbling and gurgling over the rocks and the wash of tiny waterfalls foaming over small drops and ledges.

Her heart gradually stopped its fearful pounding, and her tears slowed as a sense of peace slowly permeated the atmosphere.

Hawk sighed and trembled slightly in his release. She wanted so badly to reach out and touch him ... to feel a physical connection that might help push away the loneliness. Slowly standing, Elena took a step away from the water tank and toward Hawk. He did not move. She took another step, and his ear turned in her direction. She stopped and held a hand out toward the horse.

Please, she thought. *Can we not be closer in this life as we have been in others? We are both so alone, and while I'm happy to graze with you in the meadow, I would love to groom you and comfort you here, where we both must be for now.*

Still trembling in his exhaustion, Hawk turned his head to her and lightly brushed his muzzle whiskers against her fingers before tiredly moving a step away.

33

FEATHERS IN THE WIND

George and Sally sat on the porch swing watching the sunset fade into moonlight. They were both pleasantly tired from a day's work in the summer heat, and content to sit quietly for a while, gently rocking the swing.

"Tomorrow should be an easy day," said George. "And I'm certainly ready for a break."

Sally sighed and laid her head on his shoulder.

"You have been working hard, dear. I think a day of air conditioning and chile burgers are in order." Sally smiled and snuggled in a little closer to her husband.

George chuckled and closed his eyes, enjoying the quiet night and the closeness of his wife. His thoughts drifted to Elena.

"So how do you think our girl is doing?"

Sally thought for a minute before answering.

"I think she's adjusting incredibly well, given the circumstances. The last seven years of her life have not been easy ones."

"Do you think she is happy here?"

"I think she is content to be here, and I don't think we could ask for more than that right now. She has shown no signs of wanting to leave, and she helps around the place more than most teenagers would."

"I've been wondering if maybe she was wishing to be somewhere else the last few days," said George.

Sally had been expecting this conversation. She knew her husband had been upset and confused by some of Elena's reactions recently.

"Dear, I don't think her issues are with us. I believe she is dealing with something much deeper than being in a new foster home. Deeper than the loss of her family even."

George thought about her words for a minute.

"What do you mean? I would have thought losing her family would have been the most painful thing that could happen, and that maybe she was upset because she thought we're trying to replace them."

"Oh, I'm sure there is some truth to all of that. But I don't think that is all there is. The layers are being peeled from her like the skin of an onion. And every time a new layer is exposed, I am betting that it's as painful to her as an exposed nerve would be."

George was trying to understand, but he still was not sure where Sally was headed with this.

"What do you mean? What layers? It's obvious there is something more going on with her than I expected...." His voice trailed off.

"Elena has had to leave behind more than her home and her family. She has been torn away from her history as well. Her culture, ancestors, language, everything is gone." Sally struggled to find words to express the knowing that was in her heart. "For the past seven years it has probably felt to her as though she was living in a bubble, completely separated from the rest of humanity. Think about it, George. How many times a day do you casually think about your father when you are working in the barn that he built? Or your Grandmother and the food that she cooked when you were a boy? Recipes that were handed down in the family that might have originated in the 'Old World' before they even came to this country. How often do you notice the workmanship on a part of the house, a talent that was probably handed down through generations? How often do you look to the sky and thank God for the rain without ever giving a second thought to your belief in God and how you came by it?" Sally paused for a minute. "How many times a day do we take our homes, our land, our ancestry, and our beliefs for granted? Elena has to struggle for all of that. She only has her memories to supply her with the history and belief system of her whole culture."

George was struggling to sort through all the different thoughts and ideas that were charging through his brain like a herd of stampeding horses.

"That's why she spends so much time on the mesa at those old ruins."

"Yes," said Sally. "I think that place probably gives her a sense of history and belonging."

"So, not only are we strangers to her, but our whole world has little meaning to her," said George. He went quiet again, trying to fathom the whole depth of this idea. The hugeness of it was like trying to imagine the boundaries of space and the effort made his stomach knot up.

Well, he thought. *If just thinking about it does that to me, I can't even imagine what living with it does to Elena.*

As they sat in the quiet, contemplating their conversation, a beautiful sound filled the night air. Eerie and lilting at the same time, the music seemed overflowing with emotion. This time both Sally and George recognized the source. They looked at each other and smiled. It was Elena playing the ocarina.

After Hawk had withdrawn to the Owl Tree, Elena sat on the edge of the water tank, weak and exhausted, and felt like crying. There was so much emotion built up inside of her that she needed a way to let it out.

After thinking about it for a minute, she slipped out of the corral, quietly entered the house so as not to call attention to herself, and hurried up the stairs. In her room she had gone to the dresser and pulled out the turtle shell. Leaving the flannel wrapping behind, she went back down the stairs and out to the corral.

She decided to sit under the tree, using the stout trunk as a backrest. The hardness and substance of the tree trunk seemed to offer her strength, and it was comforting. Tilting her head back against the tree, she closed her eyes for a little bit, allowing the cool breeze of the night air to slide across her as though a gentle river was flowing around her. Bringing the ocarina to her lips, she softly blew a long gentle note that sounded like the crying of the wind.

Hawk raised his head and flicked his ears back and forth, listening to the gentle sound.

Above her, in the tree, the owl softly joined her music with a barely perceptible *whoo hoo.*

The three friends sat in the corral in the moonlight as the notes drifted like feathers on the wind. Elena felt her need to cry flow out through the flute song, taking with it much of the heaviness in her heart. She hoped that the same thing was happening for Hawk.

After a time, the music stopped and the night was still. George and Sally shook off the sleepiness enough to get up from the swing, knowing it was time for bed.

"You go on up," George said to Sally. "I'll go check on Elena, and then I'll be right behind you."

Sally nodded and walked sleepily toward the stairs. George went through the kitchen and out the door. He stopped to listen, hearing only crickets.

Maybe she's already gone up to bed, he thought.

Whoo hoo came softly from the tree in Hawk's corral. George walked over to the fence and looked up into the tree, his eyes adjusting easily to the moonlight. The owl was well hidden in the leaves and branches, but as George's eyes traveled down the trunk, he broke into a huge smile.

There at the base of the tree was Elena. She looked as though she was sound asleep. Her head was resting against the tree trunk, tilted slightly sideways. Just a few feet away from her stood Hawk, one foot cocked, relaxed and resting.

George stood still, not wanting to disturb them. Just standing there by the fence, he felt so peaceful and content.

I wish Sally could see this, he thought.

After a few minutes, he unlatched the gate and went quietly in the corral. As much as he hated to disturb the peaceful scene, he didn't really think Elena should spend the night leaning against a tree trunk. Walking softly over to her, he shook Elena gently by the shoulders. The stallion moved quietly away as the girl roused into wakefulness.

Her eyes slowly opened but it took a few seconds for them to adjust and focus on the figure standing in front of her. She had been in a deep, seemingly dreamless sleep and the waking was not welcome or easy.

"Time for bed, sleepy head," George said softly. He held out his hand and reaching up, she took it. He pulled her up from the ground and helped to steady her until she found her balance. He could see she had something grasped in her other hand. She opened her fingers slightly and they both looked at the ocarina. He nodded, smiling, and they walked quietly out of the corral, leaving Hawk to his rest.

34

RHYTHM OF THE HOOF BEATS

Elena awoke to the sun peeking over the hills and in through her bedroom window. She had slept a deep restful sleep and needed a few minutes to wake up. So even though the sun was coming up and her brain was telling her it was chore time, she snuggled down into the pillows for a few more minutes, pulling the covers up to her eyes. She could hear subtle noises coming from below, indicating that George and Sally were probably awake and beginning their day.

After just a couple of minutes, Elena felt the urge to be moving. She threw the covers back and swung her legs over the side of the bed.

Going to be another hot day, she thought as she felt the warm air on her legs. Glancing at the bed stand, she saw the ocarina lying on top of her book. When she had come up to bed the night before, she had been too tired to put it away in the dresser. The polished turtle shell sat on the book cover that displayed a photograph of a wild horse running across the sage-covered ground, its mane and tail flying. The look of the turtle shell next to that horse somehow had a pleasing quality to it, so Elena decided to leave the ocarina where it was instead of wrapping it back in the flannel and putting it away.

She could hear the kitchen door close beneath her window and knew that it was time to get moving. She had to clean and fill Hawk's water tank before they left for the sale barn.

George was loading the feed truck with hay for the cows when Elena arrived at the barn. She hurried over to the grain bins and scooped out feed for the ranch horses and for Hawk. She quickly distributed the buckets among the three horses. Then she went back through the barn, grabbed Hawk's bucket of breakfast, a scrub brush that hung on a nail by the door, and some hay.

She set the hay down, went through the gate, and gave the stallion his grain before turning to the water tank. It had algae growing in it. There had not been any recent water run off from the roof to overflow the tank. So she scrubbed it clean of dirt and algae, and dumped the stagnant water. On her way to get the hose, she fed Hawk his hay and picked up his bucket.

Finally she had the hose running and the tank filling, so she took a short break to spend a couple of minutes of quiet time with Hawk. He was chewing his hay and watching her closely. This was more activity than he was used to with his breakfast, but none of it really seemed directed at him, so he ate and watched.

"No time for our usual routine this morning, big guy," said Elena. "It's another town day, and I have to keep moving."

Hawk chewed his hay, pieces of it hanging out the corners of his mouth. *It's a settled, peaceful feeling*, she thought. *Like grazing. Not thinking about yesterday or worrying about tomorrow, just being.*

The tank was about full, so she left the corral to shut off the hydrant, then drained and rolled up the hose. She took Hawk's bucket back to the barn and saw that George about had the feed truck loaded. Setting the feed bucket in its place, she took a deep breath, gathering her courage and then turned back to the truck.

"Need a driver?" she asked George

"Are you sure?" He stepped down from the stack of hay to see her better.

"I am," she said. *Kinda,* she thought.

"Well, OK, then. That will certainly get us done a lot quicker," said George, handing her the key.

Elena got in and started the truck while he went to open the other big door and the gate to the lane. She put the truck in drive, and this time it pulled forward smoothly without a hitch or jerk. George jumped on the tailgate to ride to the top of the lane.

Once through the gate, he started calling the cattle. They had seen the truck and were already on their way.

"You know the drill, Elena. Let's go."

She shifted the truck to the lowest gear and gradually let up on the brake. Again, the truck rolled forward smoothly.

Maybe I'm getting the hang of this! She was getting more confidence and even let her left elbow rest on the door, holding the wheel with just her right hand.

"Honk the horn a few times!" shouted George from the top of the haystack. "Some of them haven't seen us yet!"

So the truck crawled along, with an occasional honk, cows running along side as George threw off the hay. Very soon they were finished and headed for the barn.

They parked the truck, closed up the barn, and made a beeline for the house and breakfast.

"Just eggs, toast, and fruit this morning," said Sally as they came through the door. "We have a big lunch ahead of us."

"Chile burgers!" said George loudly. "And a milk shake!"

They washed their hands and sat down to eat. There was little conversation since everyone was eating and thinking about the upcoming trip. Breakfast was over in ten minutes or less, and the dishes on their way to the sink.

Washed up and changed into clean clothes, they were soon in the truck and headed out the driveway.

***

The drive was uneventful. There were a few antelope in the road, so George drove slowly allowing them time to find places to crawl through the fence.

Elena watched the hawks that hunted from the wooden fence posts beside the gravel road. Some of them took off as the diesel truck approached. Others appeared oblivious to the noise and the cloud of dust that rose from the tires on the powdery dirt. Lizards ran from the edge of the road down into the bar ditch, and there was an occasional tarantula making its unhurried way through the dirt and the stones and the weeds.

Soon they were cruising down the main two-lane highway. The air conditioning was on, and everyone was comfortably clean and cool, which was unusual for this time of day at the ranch.

George's eyes scanned the horizon in the perpetual pursuit of a raincloud over the mesa or a thunderhead building in the mountains. There was no sign of anything but blue sky.

Sally pulled a CD out of the console and inserted it into the player. Soon the beautiful clear sound of classical Flamenco guitar filled the truck and serenaded them on down the road.

Elena watched the scenery flow by, and imagined herself riding down the side of the road on Hawk. In her imagination he was strong and shiny and powerful. No longer was he a skinny, unhappy misfit in the world. She could feel his muscles rippling underneath her, carrying her forward, his hoof beats matching the beat of the music. She could feel her hair billowing in the wind, as was his mane and tail.

When the truck slowed to cross the railroad tracks, Elena lost the rhythm of the hoof beats and the powerful feeling of the horse and the wind. She was again in the backseat of the pickup truck, listening to the guitar music.

35

HIT AND RUN MIRACLE

The sale was in full swing when they arrived, having been in progress for a couple of hours. It took some time to find a parking space in the dusty sale barn lot. They didn't mind having to walk aways to get to the sale ring, so George found a place next to a tree at the far end of the lot. This was perfect, as the truck would have a bit of shade when the hot afternoon wore on.

They slipped in the side door of the sale ring and found seats up in the stands. There was no need to go by the office for a buyer number since they were only there to watch.

Good, Sally thought.

The horses, goats, and sheep had already sold. There were never very many of those as these sales were mostly about cattle. There were special horse sales here several times a year. Folks came to those to buy their working horses. The few horses that went through the ring during these regular weekly sales were usually crippled, or starving, or both. She could not bear to watch that part of the sale. They had arrived late enough that there would be only cattle for the rest of the day.

And that is bad enough, she thought, scowling.

George was looking around the room to see who was there and what sort of contacts he might make that day. There was the usual assortment of buyers and traders. Some of them made their living by buying large lots of cattle for different clients. Sometimes they would buy cheap and try their hand making money at resale in another sale in a different location.

There were small-time cattle growers there looking for replacement heifers, or a new bull. And there were always a few people that just wanted to raise a handful of cattle in their yard so that they knew they had a healthy source of beef.

The bigger ranches would come in the fall during the calf run to sell their large bunches of weaned calves if they hadn't already sold privately.

There was a pretty decent turn out for this sale, thought George. *Considering the time of year. With this drought, there may be more sellers than buyers.*

The three sat and watched the sale for an hour or so. George looked at his watch and nudged Sally's knee with his own.

"It is time for that chile burger," he whispered. And as if to punctuate his statement, his stomach served up a large growl that Sally was sure could be heard throughout the room.

Sally nudged Elena's knee. "Time to eat."

They eased passed the people sitting near the aisle and headed down the steps, out of the sale ring, past the office, to the cafe.

"I guess everyone else had the same idea," said Sally, looking around at the tables, the chairs already filled with hungry souls. She was just getting ready to suggest they come back a little later when it wasn't quite so busy, when a table full of people got up and went to the cashier to pay their bill.

George made a beeline for the table. He was hungry, and he wasn't going to risk someone snagging it before he could get there. Sally and Elena followed. They sat and piled up the dirty dishes that were on the table to make it easier for the waitress to clear them away as she hurried by. She delivered food to another table and then came back with a damp rag and her pen to clean the table and take their order.

George had known what he wanted for the past twenty-four hours, so he ordered his chile burger and a large chocolate shake, giving Elena a little more time to look at the menu. She and Sally both ordered burritos since the cafe had a reputation for great chile.

George took off his Stetson and set it on the windowsill next to him. Then he tilted back in his chair, congratulating himself for his upcoming lunch and scanning the room to see who was there. He saw a man standing by the door, looking around the room. George scanned the room again and saw no empty tables. The man at the door didn't look like a regular and was not dressed like someone who worked a ranch or drove a stock truck. That piqued George's interest. He pointed the man out to Sally.

"We have an extra place here. Should we ask that fella to join us?" he waved at the man to get his attention without waiting for Sally's answer. Sally grabbed the waitress' arm as the girl sped by.

"Please tell that gentleman waiting for a table that he is welcome to sit with us if he'd like."

The waitress nodded and delivered the message. Looking relieved, the man made his way through the room jammed with tables and people.

Good thing he's skinny, thought Elena, watching the man squeeze between obstacles.

By the time the man arrived at their table, his clean-shaven face was shiny with sweat, and his neatly trimmed brown hair was damp around the edges. George was trying to figure out what line of work the man was in, but he couldn't tell from the pressed jeans, dark blue polo shirt and clean, white sneakers.

"Whew," the stranger said. "Popular place. I'm Mike. Mike Lewis. I want to thank you people. It was beginning to look like I'd have to skip lunch. You all are a life saver."

"No problem. I'm George Layton, this is my wife Sally," he motioned in her direction, "and this is Elena."

Mike shook everyone's hand and sat down.

"No thanks," said Mike as Elena tried to hand him a menu. "I had plenty of time to look it over while I was waiting." Waving at the waitress, he ordered a BLT and an ice tea.

"So, are you folks regulars here?"

"I guess you could say that," said George. "We raise cattle."

"Maybe you can help me then. I'm looking for someone that raises good quality, grass-fed beef."

George and Sally looked at each other and then at Mike.

"And I would prefer it to be grown locally. At least within the state of New Mexico."

The waitress arrived at the table with their food, just as George opened his mouth to answer. So he cleared his throat and waited for her to set everything down and leave.

"How much beef do you need?"

"No set amount. We aren't sure yet."

"Guess I need more details," said George, scrunching his eyebrows.

"Have you heard of 'The Lodge'?"

"You mean the old guest lodge up North in the mountains?" asked Sally. Now she was getting interested.

"That's the one. It was built at the turn of the century by an eccentric millionaire that moved to New Mexico for his health. He collected art, artifacts, and people," Mike smiled a little. "There were always writers, artists, and musicians staying at The Lodge back in the early days. The place suffered some during the depression. The owner was terminally ill by then, and while he did not lose all of his money, most of it went to his health care rather than The Lodge. When he died, the place was left to his son and daughter. Neither of them was interested in having the place, so they sold it, art and artifacts intact."

Mike took a bite of his sandwich and washed it down with a swallow of tea.

Elena was only partially listening to the story. There was so much going on around them in the cafe, and she was caught up in the busy energy of it. She found herself wondering about the people she saw there. There were truck drivers waiting to get their paperwork so they could start loading the trucks with cattle. Sitting with hats pushed back on their heads, they rocked back in their chairs and poured down cups of coffee. Many of them would be driving through the night to stockyards and other sale barns, so the caffeine was a staple for them.

The professional buyers gathered at a corner table that Elena guessed was the gathering table for the regulars. Every cafe seemed to have one of those.

She heard bits and pieces of conversations about who had bought, what was sold, and for how much. There was laughter and eyes rolled over who got stuck with a bad purchase and who was the new buyer that they had frozen out of the bidding that day.

There were families with little boys in boots and hats carrying ropes, hoping to grow up to be just like Daddy. Little girls in pink cowgirl hats and boots with dreams of being champion barrel racers and rodeo queens whispered and giggled.

Elena was so caught up in the goings on of the cafe, that she barely heard Mike continue on with his story.

"So the new owner is very involved with the actual operations at The Lodge. Even though she isn't from New Mexico, she has done her research on the history and on the flavor of the local areas."

Mike took another bite of his sandwich.

"This is where you come in. It's the owner's intention to make the dining room at The Lodge a place where everyone wants to eat. She is well aware of the healthy trends in food, and that much of Northern New Mexico is seriously interested in all-natural and organic food. We'd like to serve good, healthy grass-fed beef. We want it to be local, and better yet, from a ranch with some history. What can you tell me about your ranch?"

George knitted his brows again.

"I don't know. I was born there...." His voice trailed off, and he looked at his wife.

"That ranch is third generation in my husband's family," said Sally. "His grandfather came here from Texas. His grandmother was a school teacher from back East. They bought the ranch after the previous owners left during the depression, and the Double L has been in the family ever since."

"That was what I wanted to hear," Mike said, smiling from ear to ear. "As far as your previous question about how much meat do we need, I think we'll just have to feel that out as we go. I know we could only fit about ten steers worth of meat in our freezers at a time."

George frowned. "That would mean we'd have to feed the calves through the winter that we would normally sell in the fall. With this drought, that could be a deal breaker."

"We need to crunch some numbers," said Mike, looking as though he were already doing that in his head. "Maybe the amount you would make by selling your meat retail could make up for the feed you will have to buy. Do you think you'd be able to supply at least 50 steers a year?"

"Yes, that would be easy enough to do if we can figure out the logistics to everyone's satisfaction." George handed Mike a business card. "Here is our contact information. Call me if you'd like to set up another meeting."

"I'll be calling you soon," said Mike as he pushed his chair back and stood up. "Go over your numbers, think about how much per pound for the different cuts of meat you would need, and then we can get together again. I'd like to get this worked out before Fall, if possible."

George and Mike shook hands, Mike handed George a business card, then smiled and nodded at Sally and Elena.

"Nice to meet you folks. I'm looking forward to working with you."

Mike took his leave, stopping at the cashier to pay for his food and waived on his way out the door.

"Well," said Sally, a little at a loss for words.

She looked at George, who was still staring at the doorway to the Cafe.

"That seemed like what I would call a hit-and-run miracle."

"Stranger things have happened. I wonder if that guy is for real," he said, looking thoughtfully at Mike's business card.

Sally got a dreamy look in her eyes.

"If this works, we might never have to sell anything here again. Can you imagine?"

George chuckled. "Let's not get ahead of ourselves now," he said carefully. He knew that her disappointment would be terrible if this fell through, and the thought of that made him cringe.

"Why not? Why not see the positive side of this and make it work? Can you think of any reason to not follow through with this?"

"I didn't say that, dear. I just don't want to start counting our chickens before they hatch. We have a lot of work to do to see if we can make this happen."

"Well, if we are going to be practical, then we should get ourselves up from these chairs and get moving. We still need to stop at the store before we head home. Elena, have you finished your lunch?"

Elena nodded and pushed her chair back.

George stood up, put on his hat, and pulled out his wallet. He stuck a five-dollar bill under his plate and made his way through the maze of tables, chairs, and people to the cashier. Sally and Elena followed.

"Sir," said the waitress, looking at the money George was holding out to her, "That man that was sitting with you paid for your meals when he left."

George raised his eyebrows and handed the waitress an extra dollar. Sally and George looked at each other, smiling.

"OK then," said Sally. "Let's get to the truck and turn on the AC."

***

Elena smiled as she gazed out the truck window. It was after three in the afternoon and she was getting that warm day, mid-afternoon, sleepy feeling.

Interesting day, she thought. *And evidently a good day as well. The Laytons seem thrilled with the news that man brought to them at the sale barn Cafe. Not only will it be nice to not have to take their cattle to the sale barn, but if they could make it through the first year or so of having to buy extra feed, there is a good chance they will be making more money on their sales by far.* Elena hoped it would work out.

The drive home was quiet as everyone was lost in their own thoughts. George finally stuck a CD in the player because he too was getting pretty drowsy, and his wife did not seem inclined toward conversation.

Sure is getting dry, he thought. *Seems like everything that started to grow with the rain is drying into brown, crunchy fire fuel.* His stomach knotted up as thought of the summer cow pasture that had finally just started to get green, drying up again. How would they ever be able to get through the winter feeding extra calves if they couldn't even find reliable summer pasture?

As the truck turned onto the ranch road, Elena noticed a couple of dragonflies zipping around near some weeds on the side of the road. *Odd,* she thought. *There's no water here.* She squinted through the intense afternoon sun at the horizon. There, just barely showing behind the mesa, was a cloud forming. *Hmmmm,* she thought.

When they arrived at the ranch and Elena stepped out of the air-conditioned truck, she understood why the dragonflies had been out and about on what was seemingly a hot, dry afternoon. The air was thick with humidity. A sweat immediately broke out on her skin, and it was a heavy, uncomfortable feeling.

George and Sally felt it too and stood looking at the horizon.

"Is that a thunderhead building over there?" Sally asked.

"I sure hope so," George said. "Just in case, we had better get the chores done so the critters can eat before the deluge hits. Sally, maybe if you give the garden a good watering it will convince those clouds to rain on us. Maybe we should even wash the truck," he said, winking at Elena.

By the time Elena had finished feeding the ranch horses, she was dripping with sweat.

There's not one bit of breeze out here, she thought as she wiped the sweat off of her face with her shirtsleeve. *Ugh.* She scooped up Hawk's grain and grabbed a couple of flakes of hay. Passing Sally who was watering the garden and wiping at the sweat on her face, Elena carried dinner to the stallion.

Hawk was standing as still as a statue in the shade of the Owl Tree. As she carried his feed in and got closer, she could see that he too was covered in sweat. He did not seem inclined to move, even for food, so instead of putting it in the usual spot, she carried it to his shady place and set it down.

"OK, horse," she said quietly. "You need to eat, even if you are hot and miserable.

He turned his head ever so slightly to look at her, but he did not take a step toward the food.

Shaking her head, she smiled.

"Well, I am going to go get into the shade myself. I hope you change your mind and eat that dinner. You're still pretty darned skinny, and I would think you'd want your nice, shiny coat and manly muscles back." She winked at him and left the corral without looking back.

After double-checking to make sure all the gates were closed and latched and all the water tanks had plenty of water, Elena started toward the house. As she passed the stallion pen, she smiled. Hawk was standing over the feed bucket chewing slowly, grain dribbling from the corners of his mouth.

36

DELUGE AND DARKNESS

Sally had the shades in the house pulled down part way on the west-facing windows, trying to ease some of the oppressiveness from the heat. The ceiling fan in the living room lent it's whooshing rhythm to the moist, heavy air.

Elena let out a sigh of relief as she entered the dark, relative coolness of the house. Sally had come in not long before and was wiping freshly washed hands and face on a paper towel. George came in right behind Elena, and he too let out a huge sigh as he entered the comfortable cave-like kitchen.

Sally was standing in the middle of the room looking rather vacant.

"Whats up, hon?" asked George as he hung up his hat and walked to the sink.

"Oh ... I just can't figure out what to fix for supper. Nothing really sounds very appetizing."

"I think that we should just take the pitcher of water to the living room, and get comfortable and not move for a while," said George as he wiped his face. "We had a big meal at lunch, and there's no rule that says we even have to have supper. Let's go 'veg' awhile."

"What a good idea, dear," Sally said, looking tired and relieved. She went to the refrigerator and pulled out the water pitcher. She flavored the water with some lemon and mint while Elena got the serving tray and some glasses.

They all settled in their favorite spots in the living room. George in his big recliner, Sally on the sofa, and Elena stretched out on the floor, her back propped up against the old wood stove with a pile of pillows between the hard iron and her spine. They all were as still as Hawk had been earlier, moving just enough to sip their water and wipe at the sweat that popped out on their faces. There was much to talk about, but none of them seemed to have the energy for conversation.

There was discomfort in the closeness of the air, but there was much comfort in the feeling of closeness among the souls in that room, so they sat for some time in companionable silence.

Elena had no idea how long she had been dozing when the tremendous explosion of thunder made her jump, almost dumping her glass of water on the floor and leaving her heart pounding wildly. The room was darker than it had been, even though the mantel clock only read seven PM and there was a sudden strong gust of wind through the window that billowed the curtains like storm clouds.

George grinned from ear to ear and left his chair to step out on the porch.

There was no rain yet, but the sky was black with storm clouds and the wind howled through the trees and blew huge clouds of dust up the road.

Suddenly everything lit up like full sunlight, and the ground rocked with the force of the lightning strike. The thunder reverberated across the land and the moment left everyone weak-kneed and shaken.

"Wow!" breathed Sally. "That was close. I hope the animals are safe."

Elena spun around and hurried through the house to the back porch to check on Hawk. She breathed a sigh of relief to see the Owl Tree and the stallion still intact.

Whew, she thought. As much as they needed this storm, it was scary to think that one of her friends might be in danger from it. Sending encouraging thoughts to Hawk, she turned and went back to the front porch where Sally and George were still watching the progress of the storm.

"I sure hope there's some rain in those clouds," muttered George as he frowned at the sky.

Another flash of lightning came out of the clouds and a crash of thunder punctuated George's words. Just then a sheet of water came slicing out of the sky. It was as though the cloud had been carrying a huge body of water cradled within it and someone had opened a trap door, allowing it to escape all at once. Within seconds there were rivers of water rushing through the bar ditches, overflowing and creating ponds that fully covered large sections of the ranch road.

"The windows!" shouted Sally over the din of the pounding rain. "Everyone get in the house and close windows!"

Elena made a dash up the stairs, running through the rooms sliding windows closed against the storm. She intentionally did her room last, so that she could check on Hawk. She looked down into his corral, but could see nothing through the wall of water and darkness. Then the sky lit up again as bright as daylight, and for a brief moment she was able to see.

Hawk was no longer standing under the tree. It was of no help in keeping off the sheets of water, and being under it would only increase the risk of being struck by lightning. So the stallion was standing in the center of the corral, his head low to the ground, and his tail turned toward the wind.

Of main importance to Elena was that he was still standing. She breathed a sigh of relief and went down the stairs. The house was dark when she reached the living room. She stood still, waiting for the momentary confusion to clear. The house also seemed exceptionally quiet. The ceiling fan had stopped running, and all she could hear was the rain on the roof and running in the gutters. The power had gone out.

George and Sally were back on the front porch. Elena grabbed her Levi jacket and slung it over her shoulders as she stepped out the door. The temperature had dropped at least 20 degrees, and with the wind the air was down right chilly! She always marveled at how quickly things could change on this desert.

It took the thunder a few seconds to follow the next flash of lightning.

"The storm is moving," George said, squinting up at the clouds that seemed a little higher and a little lighter than moments before.

The rain was now in noticeable drops instead of one solid wall of water, and the wind had gone from the intimidating, howling menace to a lighter, cooling breeze.

As they stood on the porch they could hear the water running through the roofing gutters and down the spout to the rain barrels. After all of that lightning, George sniffed the air for smoke but could not detect any.

As the storm continued to move, the rain slowed it's rhythm but continued to fall. The darkness of night set in and the relief from the cool air sent a wave of contentment through the ranch house.

"We might as well go to bed," said Sally. "We have no lights, and the well pump isn't going to run either. If anyone feels the need for a shower, just step out in the yard for a while!"

"Well, I know I'll sleep much better without all of this dried sweat and dirt," said George, stepping off the porch, removing his shirt as he went. Almost immediately drenched, he started rubbing his chest as though he had a bar of soap.

"Come on out here, ladies. The water is fine."

Elena and Sally looked at each other. Elena dropped her jacket on the chair and they both stepped out into the rain-washed night. The shock of the cold rain hit them, and they began to laugh. George came over and slung an arm around each of them. Water was running from his short hair down his face, and he almost glowed with joy.

When they had finally absorbed enough moisture to make up for all the heat and dryness of the past couple of days, Sally headed for the house.

"You two stay on the porch for a minute. I'll run and get some towels," she said while attempting to wring some of the water out of her shirt as she went through the door.

Feeling her way in the darkness, she first grabbed a towel and stopped some of the water dripping from her hair and clothes, and then grabbed a lighter and lit some candles on her way back to the porch. Handing George and Elena each a towel, she finished drying off as best she could.

"OK, you two. Go strip out of those wet clothes, and I'll come get them as soon as I have changed." She handed George a flashlight and Elena a candle to light their way.

Elena went to her room and grabbed her sleep shirt and shorts before changing in the bathroom. *No tooth brushing or toilet flushing tonight,* she thought. She rubbed her wet hair with the towel again and ran a comb through it. The flickering candlelight reflected off of her shiny wet hair. The soft orange glow from the candle gave everything a dream-like quality that made her smile. She could imagine the ancestors sitting around their cook fires, their faces softened and glowing from the firelight. The picture seemed so real that she could almost smell the wood smoke. Her dream was chased away by a knock at the door.

"Elena, are you changed?"

She opened the door to give Sally the wet clothes.

Sally had George's wet clothes draped over her arm, along with her own.

"Good. I could use a little light, Elena. Could you bring that candle and lead the way downstairs to the laundry room?"

Elena shielded the flame with her hand to keep it from blowing out as they went down the stairs.

After putting the wet clothes in the laundry room, Sally went through the house shutting off light switches and the ceiling fan.

"It should be wonderful sleeping weather tonight," she said. "And I would hate to wake up in the wee hours to a houseful of lights and fans if the linemen happen to get this fixed before morning."

They went back up the stairs and said their good nights. George had a candle going in the bedroom, Elena closed the door to her room and set her candle on the bed stand. She went to the window and looked out into the darkness. She could barely make out shadows through the rain, but everything felt OK.

Guess I'll have to settle for that, she thought. *Won't be able to see much of anything until morning.* She poofed her pillows, slid between the cool sheets, and blew out the candle. Lying there listening to the rhythm of the rain, her mind wandered back to the ancestors. As she thought about the flames of the cook fires and the adobe bricks of the pueblo homes and the hands that ground the corn, rolled the dough, and shaped the clay pots, she could almost feel the heartbeat of the earth enveloping her and becoming one with the beating of her own heart. The scents of sage and cedar seemed to fill the air, and she felt earthy and wild. She felt comfortable, cozy, and restless all at the same time.

Unable to sleep, she left her bed to stand at the window. The rain-soaked breeze filled the room and her senses as she stood looking out into the night.

Whoo hoo, came softly from the Owl Tree.

"Whoo hoo, yourself," said Elena softly. She smiled into the dark, picturing the owl perched in the tree, watching through the rain for any motion that might become dinner.

She stood at the window a while longer, allowing herself to feel a part of what was outside of it. The Owl, the tree, Hawk, the rain-soaked earth. She could feel the mud squeezing up between her toes, and the rain running down her face and neck and the front of her shirt. A quiet, fluttering snort came from the corral, and for a brief moment she was grazing with the herd in the meadow.

That is what this feels like, she thought. *Standing here with Owl and Hawk, in the quiet, feeling the earth all around us. It is like grazing with the herd.* She smiled as the restlessness began to ease, as feeling a part of the earth became as much a comfort as it was an excitement. She stayed at the window a while longer, allowing the feeling of comfort to rock her into sleepiness. Then she went back to bed, snuggling down into the pillows and into the arms of comforting Mother Earth.

37

THE ROLL-OVER RESCUE

Elena woke to the sound like someone hammering on steel. *Crash ... bang!* Whatever it was, it was right under her window. She jumped out of bed, goosebumps on her arms from the damp cool air. Moving to the window, she looked down through the gray, predawn light. Then she grabbed her jeans and ran down the stairs as quietly as she could, but losing no time. Buttoning her jeans and cramming her bare feet into her mud boots, she charged out the door.

Slowing as she approached the stallion pen, she assessed the situation. Hawk lay on his back next to the fence. All four legs were in the air and in the fence. Evidently he had rolled in the mud, the activity he so loved, and gotten stuck against the fence. She stood still, afraid of scaring him and causing him to hurt himself further. She knew she had to do something soon. A horse cannot lie on their back for long without running the risk of their internal organs being crushed by their weight.

Mud was churned up all around the horse where he had been struggling. Now he lay still, breathing loudly. The noise that had awakened her had been his hooves banging on the metal fence as he struggled.

Slowly she opened the gate just wide enough for her to slip through. Approaching the stallion carefully, she tried to think of a plan. What would her father have done? She was going to have to try to roll him over, away from the fence, but how on earth was she going to do that without getting pawed or kicked? And was she strong enough? Even as thin and malnourished as this horse had been, he still probably weighed close to eight hundred pounds.

Hawk groaned and thrashed again, his hooves striking metal and the sound echoing in the early morning silence. Elena quickly moved forward and grabbed both front legs of the horse. She was no longer worrying about getting hurt, she was only worried about getting Hawk off of that fence. She wrapped her arms around his flailing legs and threw all her weight into pushing them away from the fence. He rocked a little on his back, and then fell back again. She threw her weight against him again and again, getting a rocking motion going. She did not notice at what point he stopped struggling against her, but finally his body began to tip away from the fence, and she flung herself toward his back end to help it follow the front over. He almost rocked back on top of her, giving a violent kick with his hind legs. At the same time, she heaved against him with all of her strength. His hooves barely missed her head, and she could feel the breeze going by her ear. And then it was over.

Hawk lay on his side, his legs on the ground away from the fence, breathing heavily, exhausted from the effort. Elena had lost her balance in the mud since all of her body weight had been pushed against him, and she fell with him, landing in a sitting position with her back against his.

It took a little recovery time before she realized that she was back-to-back with, and touching solidly, her friend. She looked him over as best she could without moving and disturbing him. Trying to see through the mud for cuts, scrapes or gouges, from where she sat, she could see no evident injury.

All was quiet except crickets, ground frogs croaking in the huge puddles, and an occasional hummer zooming out to find early morning blossoms. Elena wanted this moment to never end. Hawk seemed to be resting quietly for the moment, and she was going to stay close to him for as long as he would allow it. She tried lightly running her hand along his rib cage. He snorted and jerked his head a little, so she stopped and waited. There they stayed, listening to the croaking and chirping and occasional fly-bys from the humming birds. Hawk's breathing began to slow and quiet, and Elena knew this moment was about over.

Hawk gave a great heave, pulling his shoulders, neck, and head up and struggling to get his legs out in front of himself so that he could get up. Elena rolled away from him and struggled in the mud to get on her feet as well. Hawk rocked his weight backwards and then forward and lunged up out of the mud onto his feet. After making sure he had his balance, the stallion shook himself violently, sending mud flying in all directions.

As Elena felt herself pelted with more mud, she thought, *Great ... I am an adobe brick and the sun has not yet risen.* Then she giggled, thinking what a sight they must make standing there covered in mud. She noticed Hawk looking at her through his long, muddy forelock, his gaze intent yet peaceful at the same time. They were again in the meadow grazing. This time shoulder-to-shoulder. Partners. Friends. Then they were back in the corral, covered in mud. He continued to look at her for a few more moments, then moved to the water tank for a drink.

Elena heard the kitchen door open and saw George come out, his coffee cup in one hand, the other putting on his hat. He started for the barn, and then happened to glance at the stallion pen. She stood her ground as he came toward her, sipping his coffee as he walked.

Arriving at the corral, George rested his arms on the top rail of the fence and took another sip of his coffee. His first inclination was to laugh as he stood looking at the girl and the horse, and he couldn't stop the corners of his mouth from curving into a smile.

"Am I ever going to see you dry again?" he asked with his eyebrows raised.

Elena burst out laughing, partially in relief and partially due to the look on George's face.

"What on earth have the two of you been doing?"

"He was stuck. On the fence. He couldn't get up, so I had to roll him over."

"By yourself? Why didn't you come get us to help? It might have been a lot easier with three of us."

"There wasn't time. While I was standing here trying to figure out what to do, he started struggling and I was afraid he would really hurt himself, so I just did it."

George stood looking at the mud-soaked horse and girl. He was totally amazed that she had been able to roll that horse over by herself. There was a good chance the stallion would have struggled harder if three had approached him, but where on earth had that skinny teenager found the strength?

"Well," he said. "Looks like you're due for another trip to the laundry room. I think we should probably hose some of that mud off of you first, though. Sally will have your hide if you carry all of that dirt through the house. Good thing the power came back on during the night. The laundry is really piling up."

"Bbbrrrr," Elena sputtered as the water from the hose ran down the front of her. The sun was just beginning to filter through the left-over clouds hanging on the horizon. The air was damp and chilly, and the hose water was down right cold.

George grinned.

"Not as much fun as in the heat of the day, is it?"

He quickly finished the job. No point in making the girl sick.

"You go on to the house," he said. "I'll get everyone fed."

Elena had learned there was no point in arguing. George was perhaps more stubborn than her, so she went to the house and he ambled off to the barn, whistling a spirited tune.

Elena checked on Hawk as she passed the corral. He was standing quietly, watching the barn door, waiting for his breakfast to emerge.

Sally was bustling around in the kitchen. She stopped in her tracks when Elena came through the door.

"Lord, girl, what have you been into so early in the morning?"

"Mud," said Elena.

"No kidding. But why?"

Elena briefly explained to Sally what had happened.

"Off you go to the laundry room, then. I hope you don't run out of clean clothes before I get the washing done." Sally softened the comment with a smile.

"Is Hawk doing OK?"

Elena nodded. "Seems to be. He was looking for his breakfast when I came in."

"Well that's a good sign." Sally said. "If he was colicky from his ordeal, he probably wouldn't be so interested in breakfast."

She turned her attention back to their own breakfast, and Elena went to change.

38

WISDOM OF THE STALLION

By the time they sat down to breakfast, the sun was shining brightly, the clouds had burned off, and steam was rolling up from the ground.

"So what's on everyone's agenda today?" asked George as he stabbed a piece of salsa-covered chicken.

"Number crunching for me," said Sally. "And I will probably require your input when you are finished feeding the cattle. We need to start working on the possibility of a partnership with The Lodge."

George nodded and looked at Elena.

"I think I should drive the feed truck this morning," she said. "Then, if Hawk is still doing OK and doesn't need me, I would like to hike up to the mesa."

"I'd love to have your help this morning, Elena. Thanks!" George turned to Sally.

"When we finish with our bookwork, I want to take a quick ride up to check out the pasture. Last night's rain may have saved it from total burn-out. Want to join me?"

"Of course I do, dear. I wouldn't miss the chance to go for a ride with my husband. It's a date."

George and Sally grinned at each other like teenagers.

Elena grinned down at her plate.

They finished their breakfast, and Sally went to her desk with a stack of files containing records of past sales, cattle prices, and retail beef prices.

"Research time," she said as she sat down at her computer.

George and Elena put on their boots at the back door, grabbed their hats, and went to feed cattle.

Elena was relieved to find that the thought of driving the feed truck no longer struck fear into her heart.

This definitely gets easier every time I do it, she thought as she climbed up into the driver's seat and turned the key.

George opened the barn door and the gate, and stepped up onto the tailgate.

"OK, driver. Let's go."

She was definitely grateful for the four-wheel drive when the truck struck deep mud just inside the pasture gate. The tires spun a little, and then the front wheels grabbed a hold and did their job. Aside from the mud, the feeding went as usual, and they were soon headed back down the lane to the barn.

After parking the truck, Elena went to check on Hawk. The mud had dried in his coat, and he was a terrible mess. Aside from that he seemed fine. He had finished his breakfast and was hanging out under the tree, seemingly half asleep.

After removing her boots and hat by the door, Elena poked her head around the corner to see Sally sitting in front of her computer totally engrossed with columns of numbers, meat charts, and past receipts from sales.

An idea suddenly came to Elena, and she went up the stairs instead of interrupting Sally. The ocarina was still on top of the book that lay on the bed stand. Picking it up, she wrapped it in its protective flannel and put it carefully in her pocket. She went back down the stairs, and Sally called to her, so she turned and went to see what she wanted.

"Are you on your way to the mesa then?" asked Sally.

Elena nodded. "Yes," she answered. "Feeding is finished, so thought I'd try to get there before the worst of the heat gets us."

"Good idea. We'll see you back here in a couple of hours for lunch?"

"Yup."

"Alright then. Have a good time." Sally smiled at her distractedly and then turned back to her work.

Grabbing hat and water bottle, Elena slipped out the door and went to the stallion pen. Setting her bottle down by the gate, she went in to do a closer inspection of the stallion, wanting to make sure he was all right after his earlier ordeal.

Slowly, she walked across the corral, being careful not to look him in the eye. He was standing under the tree, watching her approach. His ears were up and alert, and he turned his head to watch her, but aside from that, he had not moved when she reached the tree. She stood, breathing shallowly, trying to not do anything that might startle him into moving away from her.

As Elena scanned the horse's legs and then body, looking for any sign of injury, she caught a movement in the tree from the corner of her eye. Something white fluttered among the leaves in the slight breeze. Then the object came loose and floated to the ground, coming to rest on a root near the trunk of he tree. She wanted to go to it, but had not yet finished her appraisal of the horse's health. So she stayed put and turned her attention back to Hawk.

He was looking at her, and the flame was flickering in his eye. They stood staring intently at each other for a long moment, and then they were standing on a mountaintop, shoulder-to-shoulder, looking down into a valley interspersed with rocks and tough grasses and hard, gravely ground. The stallion and Elena-Mare were motionless and making not a sound. As they watched, a line of horses moved out from under a rocky outcrop. These horses had riders, and the riders all had ropes and rifles. As the line of horses followed the trail behind a huge boulder, the stallion quietly nudged Elena-Mare and the two of them slipped away toward the back of the mountain. As they approached the tree line, Elena saw movement that revealed itself to be the rest of the stallion's herd. They had been hidden while he went to check on the riders.

Escape was possible, but it would need to be silent and immediate. At the stallion's insistence, the herd turned back to the trees and quietly disappeared into the forest, with the stallion and Elena-Mare following to make sure there were no stragglers.

Elena was sure that any moment they would be running madly from the mounted men, but when the herd emerged from the trees, they were on the far side of the mountain and actually heading in the opposite direction from the danger. All was quiet.

They were back in the corral ... the mud encrusted, scrawny horse, and the fascinated girl, still staring at each other. Elena was amazed at how the wisdom of the stallion had lead his herd to safety in the other world.

Hawk snorted, shook his head as if to say, "all in a day's work", and sauntered over to the water tank for a drink.

As she watched him walk across the corral, her eyes fell on the feather at the base of the tree. Walking to it for a closer look, she saw that Owl had left a gift. The feather was mostly white with misty tan and gray stripes. Since it had been hung in the tree until just a few minutes ago, it was completely clean and in almost perfect shape.

Silently thanking Owl, Elena braided the feather into her hair.

"Horse, " she said. "I must get going if I am to be back for lunch."

Hawk snorted and walked back to his tree to stand, looking out at the horizon.

Elena slipped through the gate, picked up her water bottle, and struck out across the driveway to the forest trail. The trail and the climb had become so familiar to her that she paid little attention, except for trying to be aware of snakes and cacti. Her mind was still wandering a bit in the other world. How different this last visit had been to the ones of a couple of nights ago that had left her so terrified and drained.

39

TRAVELING IN TWO WORLDS

There was a light, relatively cool breeze blowing when she reached the mesa top. She was amazed at how different it looked, and it seemed as though years had passed since she was last there, instead of just days. There was green native grass popping up from between rocks and from under cactus and trees. It rippled in the wind as though waving to her and welcoming her back. There were blooms of bright red and pale yellow on most of the cactus plants. White and purple wildflowers were scattered everywhere, and the pinion trees were becoming plentiful with pine cones that would one day yield the pinion nuts that birds, squirrels, and humans so loved.

Obviously rain had reached the mesa, and true to form, the desert had flowered in gratitude. As Elena stood admiring the mesa, the eye appeared in her mind, the flame burning bright with reflection. As she tried to see what the eye was showing her, a small herd of horses appeared in front of her, scattered out across the mesa, grazing in the native grass. These horses appeared smaller than what she was used to seeing, almost stunted. They paid her no attention as she turned to head to the ruins. Feeling as though she were traveling in two worlds, she wound her way through the trees looking for the path she knew so well. Not being able to find the path didn't really bother her. She knew her way around on this mesa.

She heard the sounds long before she reached her destination, and as she approached the forest's edge, she was only a little surprised to see that the ruins were not ruins. The village was intact and in good shape. There were people quickly but quietly moving in and out of the buildings. It appeared that things were being gathered and readied for a journey and there was nothing in the stack of items that was too large to be carried easily by one person. The people communicated in hushed tones in a language that she was not familiar with, but seemed to understand. The men were continually looking out across the canyon to a ledge on the far side.

Elena squinted into the sun trying to see what they were looking at. A flash caught her attention. It appeared to be sunlight reflecting off of something shiny. As her eyes adjusted to the bright sunlight, she could see a line of riders on horses. They were so far away that they looked like a line of ants, but they were not insects, they were soldiers.

The people continued, readying to leave. They did not seem panicked however. The women gathered up the children and the household items that they could carry. The men gathered weapons. Spears and arrows and bows. Rock blades and hammers lashed to wooden handles, extra arrowheads made from finely chipped and crafted stones.

As Elena watched, she wondered if she were as a ghost to the people as she had been before, or if she were a part of the scene, as with the horses. She didn't have to wait long to find out. One of the women hurried over to her and grabbed her arm, pulling her to the stack of household items, and slung water bottles lashed with leather straps over her shoulders and motioned for her to follow.

As if carefully orchestrated, the people all at once went into the forest, carrying what they could and herding the children ahead of them. As they did, they spread out and disappeared into the trees. A picture of the wild horses doing the same flashed through her mind. She stepped carefully and quickly since she knew her way through this forest. When she emerged on the other side at the opposite rim of the mesa, she was alone. The herd of horses was gone, and the people had vanished. She looked for the water bottles that had hung around her neck, but all she saw was the owl feather that she had braided into her hair that morning, fluttering in the breeze.

Elena listened for any sound that might give her a clue to what was happening and to what world she was in at the moment. Hearing nothing but the wind, she sighed.

I am going to have to go back there to see what's happening, she thought. She did not relish the idea of possibly coming upon an army of soldiers bent on destroying her people, but she did not know what else to do since every tell-tale sign had disappeared.

Moving swiftly and as silently as possible, Elena went through the juniper and pinion forest again. As she approached the forest edge, she slowed to a creep, sneaking to a large tree and shielding herself with it, peeked out at the village. Or what used to be the village. It was ruins again. Not freshly ruined by an army of soldiers, but ancient ruins. Elena quickly calculated in her head. Those had been Spanish soldiers, so the people had left this place four or five hundred years ago. She emerged from her hiding place in the trees and walked out to the center of the ruins. Standing there gazing around her, she could imagine a little bit of what it must have been like living here then. She could also imagine how horrible the scene would have been if the people had not seen the Spanish coming and had not had the wisdom to quietly retreat and vanish.

40

FINDING HER FUTURE IN THE PAST

A breeze lifted the owl feather in her hair, and she smiled and looked toward the base of the foundation where she had buried the arrowhead with the horsehair and hawk feather attached. Something fluttered there, and she smiled in anticipation as she went to the object and knelt down. The gift had survived the storm. The rust red feather was a little battered, but it was all intact in Hawk's tail hair braid. Reaching up, she unbraided her own hair and retrieved the owl feather. Smiling a little, she attached the owl feather next to the hawk feather in the braid. Then she sat back on her heels and listened. There was still no sound other than the wind. No chattering, scolding jays, no violent visions like she had had on previous visits, and no shadow. Standing, Elena pulled the ocarina from her pocket and unwrapped it. She stuffed the flannel back into her pocket and looked down at the feathers. A shadow passed over the gift, startling her. With her heart in her throat, she looked up to see a hawk soaring gracefully, in huge circles, riding the gentle winds.

Still watching the hawk, she put the flute to her lips and blew a long, graceful, haunting note, and then another. The music seemed to dance on the wings of the great bird, soaring and spiraling in time with the wind. She closed her eyes to feel the music and the dance. Then another, deeper flute joined in. Startled, she opened her eyes to see her father sitting in the shade of the adobe wall that had surrounded Sam's corral, playing his larger ocarina with the deep voice that seemed to fill the universe. And even more startling was the little girl sitting next to him, playing the smaller ocarina that he had made for her.

Elena did not know how to handle this dream. In all of the other dreams and visions she had experienced, she had always been herself. Sometimes she had been herself as a horse, and sometimes as herself centuries ago, and sometimes as herself as a witness to what was happening, but she had always been Elena.

Now she might still be Elena, but she was looking at herself, Elena, as a child years ago.

Am I real in this world? she wondered. *Can they see me? How can I be real when I a standing right in front of myself?* Stepping forward to get closer to them, she saw Elena-Child smile as she played. Also continuing to play, Elena looked at her father. His deep-voiced ocarina sang its haunting tune, and a tear slid from his eye as he looked at his almost grown daughter.

A figure came out the open door of the adobe cabin behind them, and Elena's mother walked down to the wall to listen to the music. She too had a tear trickling down her cheek.

The three ocarinas played beautiful harmony while Sam the old Appaloosa stood next to the wall with a look of total contentment.

Then her father put down his flute and stood up. Taking her mother by the hand, and grasping Sam's halter with the other, the three of them walked quietly away, leaving Elena-Child alone with Elena.

"No," she tried to call to them while the child continued to play. "No ... don't go!"

But the words had no sound, and father, mother, and Sam disappeared into the horizon. The little girl continued to play with tears streaming down her cheeks. Elena put her ocarina to her lips and played harmony to the little girl's music. They both cried.

Elena closed her eyes in an effort to stop the tears, but it didn't work, and when she opened them, she was alone with the hawk on the mesa, still playing to the wind.

Putting the turtle shell back in its flannel, she sat against the ruined foundation and sobbed. She sobbed for what seemed like an eternity, crying for her parents and for Sam and her brother. She cried for the child that had been left alone. She cried for her people who had so much of their history stolen from them and had to walk away with only themselves and what they could carry, generation after generation. She cried for her people that had been murdered, just as the herds of horses and buffalo had been. She cried for the stallion, Hawk, who had lost his family and was alone in the world.

The more she cried, the more she felt like the tears would never stop. Then Hawk's eye came into her mind. Even though there was a large, single tear coming from the corner of the eye, the flame still flickered. Looking into that flame, she could see everything. Hawk was there, and Owl, while redtail still circled overhead. She could see the ranch horses standing together under their tree. Sally was working in her garden, and George was fixing a loose board on the hay barn.

And she saw the little girl, with her father and mother, walk toward her. The little girl held out her hand to Elena as she looked back at her parents and waved. They held hands and walked, and Elena found herself telling the child about everything that had happened since the accident. The child listened and nodded and they tightened their grips on each other's hands. When the stories ended, so did the dream.

Elena sat contemplating the feathers. She felt totally drained, but she also felt totally emptied. Emptied like a vessel that had been relieved of its contents and then washed clean, ready for a new job. She had gone into the past and found herself. Now she needed to move into the future. There was still much about the past that needed to be understood, dealt with, and healed where possible. How could she go about such a huge challenge? She had no answers for sure, but she was beginning to realize that she wasn't completely alone in the world, even if none of her new family had any knowing about her past or her people, maybe they would be able to help her find it. Hawk had certainly been instrumental in walking her through the past, present and future in a way she could never have imagined.

My mother knew! She knew all of this. It is what she's been teaching me since I was born. This thought so comforted her. She had been following the teachings all of this time. She had not completely lost her heritage. This was something. It was a place to start. This knowledge could take her into the past and the future if she could just find the wisdom to follow.

Exhausted and realizing that Sally would be worrying about her again, she got to her feet and started back to the ranch.

41

FROM THIS PLACE FORWARD

When Elena arrived back at the ranch, she was surprised to see that there was no sign of activity. *The Laytons must be inside getting ready for lunch,* she thought. So she went to the house. Stepping into the kitchen, she expected to see Sally preparing lunch and George washing up, or leaning against the doorframe telling Sally about his morning. But the kitchen was empty and clean.

Odd, thought Elena. *It's almost like the feeling on the mesa when the ruins turn into a living village.* She laughed at herself then, thinking, *If I had gone that far back in time here, there wouldn't be a house where I'm standing.*

Chuckling quietly, she walked through the kitchen and peeked into the office. Sally and George were sitting next to each other at the desk. Their heads were almost touching as they bent over a stack of folders, and they were deep in discussion. She glanced up at the clock and saw that it was almost one o'clock, and definitely time for lunch.

Normally George would have been growling for food long before that time, so whatever they were doing was obviously terribly important.

Elena went quietly back to the kitchen and looked in the refrigerator to see what was available for lunch. She pulled some salad greens out, along with some of Sally's garden-fresh mini tomatoes and a couple of hard-boiled eggs. Pulling a large bowl out of the cupboard, she set to making a salad, hoping by the time that was done, Sally would arrive to tell her what she had planned for the meal.

She finished making the salad, put some plastic wrap tightly over the bowl and put it back in the Fridge to stay fresh. She listened carefully to hear if anyone was coming from the office, but all she heard were voices murmuring.

Hhmmm, she thought, *OK then, I'll have to figure something out. They're obviously very caught up in whatever they are doing.*

She pulled a package of tortillas, some cheese, and some left-over chicken from the refrigerator. Putting a tortilla on each plate, she grated cheese on each of them, and then chopped the chicken into small pieces and sprinkled it on the cheese. On top of the chicken she put some chopped onion and green chile. Slipping the plates in the oven to melt the cheese, she set the table, found a bottle of salsa, and got out the pitcher of water and glasses. As she was pulling the plates from the oven, a large oven mitt on each hand, Sally and George came through the door from the hallway.

Elena was glad to see they both looked surprised and then pleased. This was the first time she had taken the initiative to do something like this without being asked or told, and she hadn't been sure how it would be received.

"Elena," said Sally. "We never even heard you come in, and here you have fixed a whole meal while we were buried in our paperwork."

"Thank goodness," said George. "I am starving!"

"Go wash up," Elena grinned her relief and carried the warm plates to the table. "Lunch is ready."

"Well dear, what do you think our chances are of making this 'Lodge' deal work?" Sally asked her husband as she poured dressing on her salad.

"You saw the numbers. It sure won't be easy. But if we continue to get rain, it might be possible. I think we should move the cattle to summer pasture next week and start looking into sources for hay." George took a large bite of his cheese quesidilla. "What do you think, Elena. You up for a cattle drive?"

Her mouth was full, but she managed to nod enthusiastically.

"Sally and I are going to ride up and have a good look at the feed on that pasture after lunch. Want to go?"

"I think I'd like to stay here, if you don't mind. I want to spend some time with Hawk, and do you think I could use the computer for a little research?"

"Elena! I'm so sorry," said Sally. "I never even thought about it. You should have your own e-mail account."

"Oh, that's OK. I don't know who I would e-mail. But there are some things I would like to look up online."

"Of course. The Internet is a little slow way out here. But if you have the patience, you are more than welcome to use the computer. Do you have something special in mind?"

"I thought I might look up some things about my home and my people. Maybe some history and some information about my family."

George looked bothered by what Elena was saying, but Sally was pleased.

"What a good idea. I'll be interested to hear about your findings."

When lunch was finished, Elena shooed George and Sally out of the house.

"I'll take care of the dishes. You two go ahead and go."

Sally wondered briefly why Elena seemed anxious to get them out of the house. But she decided not to dwell on it, remembering the last time she had gotten all worked-up over imagined issues with the girl. She and George would have their "date" for the afternoon, and she was going to enjoy it!

Elena finished cleaning up the kitchen, and saw the Laytons ride out through the forest gate.

Then she spent about an hour on the computer. She Googled her parents, but didn't find much there. Just the news story about the accident, their obituaries, and some possible ancestry leads if she were to join that genealogy website.

Then she found the tribal website and spent quite a bit of time there looking at pictures of familiar places and reading about the gatherings and news about the people. She started looking into the history of the area and the land, but finally lost patience with the slow computer and decided to go see Hawk.

Putting on her cap and shoving her work gloves into her back pocket, Elena went out the door and started for the stallion corral.

Then she stopped to listen, because there were birds making quite a racket. The ravens were busy scolding something, and the smaller birds seemed busy scolding the ravens.

She scanned the area around the barn. Everything seemed in place. She scoped out the stallion pen; nothing moving there.

The ravens continued their raucous racket, so she followed the sound to the back of the barn and up the lane to the cow pasture gate. To the left of the gate was the huge stock tank for the cattle, and the windmill that powered the pump to fill it with water. She looked all around the base of the tank and in the water and saw nothing out of the ordinary. The ravens continued their squalling, and she looked up to scold them, and then froze. On the top of the windmill tower was a huge golden eagle. The giant bird was sitting quietly, completely ignoring the screaming ravens.

Elena could feel her heart pounding in her chest as she stood glued to the spot, head tilted back, gazing at the great bird. Looking up the tall tower to the enormous bird at the top made her feel ten years old again, and she could again see herself holding hands and walking with her child self.

The huge bird spread its wings then, creating a shadow at Elena's feet, and launched itself from the tower. As the huge wings rose to catch the air, a feather came loose and floated on the breeze. The eagle rose higher, flying toward the shelter of the forest trees, while the feather softly danced on the air currents.

She stood, mesmerized, watching the eagle fly away. Only after the bird had disappeared into the trees did Elena shake herself out of her dream, allowing the little girl to follow the eagle into the forest. Turning to walk back to the barn, Elena noticed something floating on the water in the stock tank. She went to the edge of the tank and leaned as far as she could to reach the eagle feather that gently rocked on the tiny ripples created by the breeze. The tips of her fingers barely reached far enough to just pinch the end of the feather and draw it to her.

Holding the perfect wing feather, she looked back at the place where the eagle had disappeared into the trees. Then she looked down the slope to the ranch buildings. Hawk was standing under his tree, looking up toward her. She had the feeling of grazing with the herd again, and she felt surrounded by excitement and peace at the same time.

Her mind was flooded with pictures of her childhood home, the land, and its people as she walked down the lane and over to Hawk's corral. She and the stallion stood looking at each other, and he again shared his world with her. They grazed, shoulder to shoulder in the green meadow, surrounded by the herd, the river tumbling and laughing its way down the mountain.

"So, horse," Elena said as she studied the eagle feather, "we can always find our past in our dreams and our journeys together. But perhaps in this reality, this ranch is now our home, and all of us that live here are family. Maybe we are meant to move into our future together, from this place forward.

Then a thought crossed her mind, along with a picture that made her grin.

"And maybe George and Sally would like to graze with us."

ACKNOWLEDGMENTS

With all my heart, I wish to thank:

Mom and Margo for decades of telling me to "Write it Down".

M.J. ... Without you, I would never even have thought about becoming a writer.

Paula ... You have been a great source of inspiration and support since the inception of this project and throughout the process of bringing *Wild Spirits* into the world.

My awesome friends, Robin, Ellen, Bessie and Diane for providing great emotional support and creative inspiration.

Phaedra and The Writer's group for their wonderful, constructive and helpful advice.

Bessie, Ellen, Melanie and Bill for their beautiful reviews of this novel that appear on my website www.annclemons.com.

Tony Stromberg for his generosity in allowing me to use his beautiful photographic equine art on the front cover. www.tonystromberg.com

Robert Mirabal ... The creator of the turtle shell ocarina pictured on the back cover of *Wild Spirits*. www.robertmirabal.com

Lucid Design Studios for their enormous help and support throughout the editing process of *Wild Spirits*, as well as their creative design and technical prowess in preparing this novel for publication.

And Allen, who always knew I could write a book....

77432764R00132

Made in the USA
Columbia, SC
29 September 2017